The Blue Lantern

Also by Victor Pelevin

OMON RA

THE YELLOW ARROW

The
Blue Lantern

And Other Stories

Victor Pelevin

Translated from the Russian by Andrew Bromfield

A NEW DIRECTIONS BOOK

Published by arrangement with Harbord Publishing Limited, 58 Harbord
Street, London SW6 6PJ, and the Watkins/Loomis Agency

Designed by Semadar Megged
Manufactured in the United States of America
New Directions Books are printed on acid-free paper
First published clothbound in 1997
Published simultaneously in Canada by Penguin Books Canada Limited

Library of Congress Cataloging-in-Publication Data
Pelevin, Viktor.
    [Short stories. English. Selections]
    The blue lantern and other stories / by Victor Pelevin;
translated from the Russian by Andrew Bromfield.
        p.   cm.
    Contents: News from Nepal—Hermit & Six-Toes—Crystal world—
Nika—Mid-game—The life and adventures of Shed Number XII—
Blue lantern—Tambourine of the Upper World.
    ISBN 0-8112-1370-6 (alk. paper)
    1. Pelevin, Viktor—Translations into English.   I. Bromfield,
Andrew.   II. Title.
PG3485.E38A23   1997
891.73'44—dc21
                                                                    97-24808
                                                                    CIP

New Directions Books are published for James Laughlin
by New Directions Publishing Corporation
80 Eighth Avenue, New York 10011

Table of Contents

The Blue Lantern

News from Nepal

WHEN THE DOOR AGAINST which Lyubochka was pressed by the invisible force finally opened, it turned out that the trolley was already moving and now she had to jump straight into a puddle. Lyubochka jumped, but clumsily, splashing cold slush on the hem of her coat, and she didn't need to look to see what she'd done to her boots. Struggling up onto the narrow divider she found herself between two streams of huge trucks, which roared past her, spattering up a mixture of mud, sand, and snow. There was no traffic light, because there was no crossing, and she had to wait for a gap to appear in the sheer unbroken wall of tall truck bodies, the metal ones with peeling paint and crudely welded ribs, and the wooden ones frightening beyond description. The sight of the trucks streaming by interminably was so oppressive that it was impossible to imagine what senseless and cruel will could possibly be organizing the movement of these oil-spattered horrors through the grey November fog that covered the entire town. It was hard to believe that human beings could be responsible.

Finally spaces began to appear in the solid wall of trucks. Lyubochka pressed her plastic bag to her chest and stepped delicately onto the surface of the road, trying to place her feet on the black spots of asphalt among the freezing mud. On the other side of the road she saw the yellow fence of the trolley park with its tall black gates. They were usually locked by half past eight, but one side was still open and she could just slip through.

"And where d'you think you're going?" shouted a sassy woman in a sleeveless orange vest, standing by the gate holding a crowbar in her hand. "Don't you know you're supposed to go in through the lodge if you're late? Director's orders."

"I'll be quick," Lyubochka mumbled, trying to walk past her.

"I can't let you," the woman said with a smile, setting herself squarely in the way. "You can't. Try getting here on time."

Lyubochka looked up at the woman standing there, her side propped against the crowbar as it rested on the asphalt, her plump hands crossed over her belly. Her thumbs were circling around each other as though she was winding some invisible thread on them. She was smiling the way Soviet people were taught to smile in the sixties, with that hint that everything would turn out okay, but she blocked the entrance very effectively. On her right was the hut with the plywood board for visual propaganda, showing three figures embracing against the background of a map of Eurasia: there was a man with a black visor over his face carrying a strange-looking weapon; a scientist staring out with a cold and unfriendly expression, dressed in a white overall and cap; and a girl in striped Asian costume, looking oddly out of place. A strip of plywood was nailed up above the board, with the inscription:

ATTENTION! ABANDON ROBES, YOU ARE
ENTERING AN INDUSTRIAL PREMISES! DO
NOT FORGET TO PUT ON YOUR OVERALLS!

Lyubochka turned and walked towards the lodge. She had to walk round the corner of a big tall building (the windows on its first three floors painted over—they said it housed some sort of secret institute) and then along the yellow fence to a grey brick building decorated with signs bearing the mysterious abbreviations "UPTM," "ASUS," and something else in black on a brown background.

Inside, down one branch of the corridor, beside the small windows of the cash office, the drivers were chuckling in dense clouds of smoke. Lyubochka went out through another door into the park's huge yard, which was already empty and resembled an abandoned airport. There was not a single person to be seen in the space between the cyclopean structures of the work-bays and the gates which Lyubochka had attempted to walk through three minutes earlier, except for a tall man with high, wide cheekbones, wearing a red apron. On his poster he was striding straight towards Lyubochka, his muscular pink hands bearing a board with the inscription "REINFORCE DEMOCRACY!"—and if you looked closely, the vague mish-mash behind the figure turned out to be an army of countless numbers of workers, including even a few blacks. This poster which had been hanging on one of the bays had been produced in the paint shop in spring, and Lyubochka had long ago become used to it greeting her every morning. The poster was cunningly constructed so that the text of the appeal could be changed by hanging a new piece of board on two hooks. At first it had been "REINFORCE LABOR DISCIPLINE!" and then, during a period of political uncertainty, "REINFORCE THE HONOR OF LABOR!" But now, just before the holiday, they were hanging up a slogan that Lyubochka had not seen before.

She reached the door of the administrative building and went up the stairs to the first floor, to the technical department where she had been working for over two years as a rationalization engineer.

A mirror hung in the corridor, between the Board of Honor and the rack of photographs of employees who had spent time in the sobering-up station, and Lyubochka stopped to take a look at herself.

She was small, dressed in a black fake-fur coat and a blue knit hat embroidered with a red zigzag. Her face was slightly monkeyish, born wearing a frightened expression, and when she

smiled you could see the effort she was making, as if performing
the closest act to work that she was capable of.

Unbuttoning her coat (under it there was a white blouse with
a broad black stripe on the chest) and pressing herself up against
the mirror to let two workmen in padded jackets by, she got a
close-up view of her own powdered face with the distinct wrinkles around the eyes. Twenty-eight was twenty-eight, after all. It
wasn't so easy anymore to play the young girl fluttering along the
corridor like some animated rubber plant, a resting place for male
eyes made weary by the sight of large-scale metal objects.

She smiled once again into the mirror and pulled open the
door with the plaque that said "Tech. Dept." Her desk was in the
corner, by the pinpricked drafting board. Sitting behind it now,
staring her straight in the eye, was the park's director, Shushpanov, resembling a bloated, older version of the worker on the
poster. He was holding a small, brightly colored flag he had taken
out of the old Chinese vase where Lyubochka kept her pens and
pencils. She got the flag one day when the entire technical department was taken away from work to greet some exotic presi-
dent or other. Everyone was given flags and told to wave them
when the cars appeared. Lyubochka kept hers as a souvenir because it had a special, optimistic kind of glossy finish. When she
came in, Shushpanov twirled her amulet between his fingers so
fast that the two triangles above his hand were transformed into a
blurred red cloud.

"Good morning, Lyubov Grigorievna," he said formally in a
repulsively gallant fashion. "Delayed, were you?"

In reply Lyubochka mumbled something about the subway
and the trolley, but Shushpanov interrupted her.

"I'm not saying you're late. I'm just saying you were delayed.
I understand. Things to be done. The hairdresser's, the haber-
dashery shop. . . ."

He acted as though he actually was saying something nice to
her, but what frightened her most was the formal way he called
her Lyubov Grigorievna. This made everything he was saying ex-

tremely ambiguous, because it was one thing if Lyubochka was late, but if Rationalization Engineer Lyubov Grigorievna Sukhoruchko was late, that was another thing altogether.

"How are things?" asked Shushpanov.

"All right."

"I'm talking about work. How many rationalization proposals are there?"

"None," Lyubochka replied, then she frowned, wrinkling her brow, and said, "No, I'm wrong. Kolemasov from the tin shop was in, he's thought up some new improvement. For the big shears. For cutting the tin sheets. I haven't done all the paperwork yet."

"I see. And how many last month?"

"There were two. They've already been paid."

"Aha."

The director put down the little flag, spread his fingers, touching the tips together in front of his chest, and rolled his eyes, sucking in his lips and pretending he was adding up figures.

"Twenty roubles. Well, and how much do we pay you?"

He answered his own question: "A hundred and seventy. Take away twenty and the answer is one hundred and fifty. Do you get my drift?"

Lyubochka did. She not only understood what the director was getting at, she understood a lot of other things he probably wasn't thinking about at all. She felt, like spotlight beams, the gaze of the director and the gaze of the technical section chief, Shuvalov (who stared out from the small adjoining room he had made into an office), as well as the gaze of everybody else. So as not to be frozen at the very focus of the labor collective's sadistic curiosity, she turned, hung her plastic bag on the coat hanger, and began slowly taking off her fur coat.

"Therefore," said the director, "today you will make the rounds of all the shops and tomorrow you will tell me how well you've done. I would advise you to do well."

He got up from behind the desk, walked past Lyubochka's

motionless figure by the coatrack, crossed himself with slow, sweeping gestures in front of the color photograph of a ZiU-9 trolley hanging in the corner, and left the room.

Without looking at anyone, Lyubochka sat on the seat still warm from the director's backside (he'd probably been waiting ten minutes), and put her hand into the bottom drawer of the desk. No one in the room said a word; they glanced at Lyubochka, who had hidden her face behind the stack of drawers, and tried hard not to show the enjoyment they were feeling. In fact their faces expressed the opposite feeling, a vague sympathy mixed half-and-half with a sense of civic responsibility.

"Now there's an interesting thing!" said Mark Ivanovich Mennizinger, evidently deciding to break the oppressive silence.

"What's interesting?" asked Tolik Purygin, looking up from his drawing.

"This morning we brought over the throttle, so it wouldn't get dusty, and I got this interesting idea. . . ."

Mark Mennizinger stopped speaking, and Tolik realized he was waiting to be asked what the idea was.

"What idea was that, Mark Ivanovich?"

"I'll tell you. Electric current can't flow through air, right?"

"Right."

"But if you break a wire carrying a current, what do you get?"

"A spark. Or an arc. It depends on the inductance."

"Right. So electric current can flow through air after all, right?"

"What about it?" Tolik asked patiently.

"The point is that at first the current behaves as though nothing has changed. It thinks it's still flowing along the wire, after all air has no . . . no . . ."

"No charge carrier," Tolik prompted.

"Yes. That's it. So when the wire is already broken—"

"In the first place," said Shuvalov, coming out of his room, "electric current doesn't think. That's not its nature. And in the second place, when a current flows through gas, ionization occurs and charged particles are produced. That much I do know."

He switched on the wall radio, adjusted the volume, and went back into his office. A crowd of invisible balalaika players swept into the room, playing in a way sure to dispel instantly any doubts ever felt by anyone sitting there in the technical department concerning the existence of profound and truly national works for the balalaika orchestra.

Meanwhile, Lyubochka had finally convinced herself that she could control her facial muscles. She smiled several times behind the desk, then lifted her head, looked around, pulled out the applications file, and set about studying the proposed innovation: "*. . . consists in equipping the bar of the metal-cutting shears with a set of variable weights, so that it is possible by means of a simple operation to adjust the shearing movement applied. . . .*"

She screwed up her eyes for a second, the way she always did when she didn't understand something, and decided she would have to go to the tin shop and take a look at the innovation on-site. Still not looking at anyone, she stood up, opened the closet, took out a brand-new padded jacket with a folded paper sticking out of the pocket, and went out into the corridor.

Outside it was even messier than before. Large snowflakes had begun falling. When they hit the asphalt, they soaked up water, but they didn't melt completely, so the yard was quickly covered with a layer of cold, semi-transparent slush, while the air was filled with the frenzied, driving bleating of balalaikas. Pausing beneath an overhang, Lyubochka threw the jacket over her shoulders (in order to distance herself from the workers, she never put her arms into the sleeves), put on a businesslike face, and set off towards the man in red soaring high above the yard.

There were two men standing about twenty-five yards from the work-bay. At first Lyubochka thought one of them was from the cafeteria, but when she got closer, she stopped dead. The clothes she had taken for white kitchen uniforms were in fact long white nightshirts, and that was all the men were wearing.

One of them was fat and short, already past middle age, and the other was a young man with his head shaved clean. They were holding hands as they studied the poster.

"Note," the short one was saying, steam rising from his mouth, "the complexity of the conception. How mysterious it already is, a poster showing a man carrying a poster! If we develop this idea to its logical conclusion, and place in the hands of the man in the red overalls a board with a picture of himself carrying the same poster, what do we have?"

The young man glanced round at Lyubochka and didn't answer. "It's all right, she doesn't matter," said the short man, and he winked at Lyubochka, giving her a sudden vague feeling of hope.

"We have a model of the universe, that's obvious," answered the young man.

"Don't overdo it," said the short man, and he winked at Lyubochka again. "I think what we have is something like the corridor between two mirrors, which you've got yourself into again, though you didn't have to. Have you any idea where you are now?"

The young man shuddered and stared all around.

"Remember? Right, then, how did you get yourself here?"

"I remember," the young man said in a guilty voice, "I wanted to learn the meaning of death."

His companion frowned. "How many times do I have to tell you: Don't get ahead of yourself! But since you're already here, let's introduce a little clarity. Imagine that each of the infinite sequence of posters corresponds to a separate world, like this one. And in each of them there is a yard just like this one, and these . . . mammoth stalls. . . . Young lady, what are they called?"

"They're work-bays," said Lyubochka. "Aren't you cold?"

"Not at all. He's dreaming all of this. That's right then, work-bays, and there is someone standing in front of each one of them. Then the place where we are standing now would simply be one of these worlds, and we'd see—"

"We'd see . . . we'd see . . . Oh God!"

The young man screamed, threw up his hands, and ran towards one of the bays. His companion swore and dashed after him, turning as he ran to apologize to Lyubochka with a gesture of splayed hands. They both disappeared round the corner.

"Some sort of freaks," Lyubochka muttered, and walked on. As she approached a gate cut in a huge work-bay door, she had already forgotten all about them.

In the tin shop, a small space with a high ceiling, it was quiet and shadowy. Towering up in the center was a table with a tin top which was cluttered with metallic off-cuts of various colors. Three men were sitting by the wall, on two benches set at a right angle. They were playing dominoes, hardly speaking a word, placing their dominoes on the table with restrained, economical movements, and occasionally commenting on the latest move. On the table, beside the domino box, stood a packet of Georgian tea, several boxes of lump sugar, and three cups made out of skulls, with tea-leaves stuck to their yellow walls. Lyubochka went over to the players and said in a cheerful voice:

"Hello, Comrade Kolemasov! I thought I'd come over and see you."

"Hi," replied a man with a wrinkled face, sitting at the edge of the group. "How's life for the young these days?"

"Not too bad, thank you," said Lyubochka. "I've come on business. About the rationalization proposal."

"What, have you brought the money, then?" Kolemasov asked, digging his elbow into the ribs of the man next to him, who smiled.

"It's too soon for the money," said Lyubochka. "We have to do the paperwork first."

"Then go on and do it. Just a minute. . . . We'll show it to you. . . ."

Kolemasov put down a domino on the table, and that obviously finished the game. His partners shuffled on their seats, sighed, and threw down the dominoes they were still holding.

Kolemasov stood up and went over to a workbench, nodding his head for Lyubochka to follow him.

"Look," he said, "let's say we have to cut a piece of duraluminum." He dragged a silvery triangle out of a pile of off-cuts and set it in the open jaws of the shears. "Try it."

Lyubochka put her notebook on the table, took hold of the yard-long pipe welded to the handle of the shears, and pulled it downwards. But the duraluminum was obviously too thick, the handle moved down just a bit and then stopped. "It won't go any further," said Lyubochka.

"Right. So now what we do is this." Kolemasov picked up a thirty-pound weight from the floor and carried it over to the shears, turning scarlet in the face; then he lifted it to chest height and hung it on the handle.

"Try pressing it now."

Lyubochka pressed down with all her weight on the pipe. It moved a little further and then stopped again.

"You have to press harder than that," said Kolemasov, and he pressed on the handle himself. It moved slowly downward and suddenly the sheet of duraluminum flew apart with a crack, the handle jerked, the weight jumped off it and thudded heavily into the tiled floor just to the left of Lyubochka's boot.

"That's the improvement," said Kolemasov.

His two domino partners followed what was happening with interest.

"I see," said Lyubochka. "But it says here that you have a set of changeable weights."

"Haven't got them yet," answered Kolemasov. "But the idea's simple. You have to have several weights. You hang them on one at a time, or two or three together."

Lyubochka began trying to think up an intelligent question.

"Can you tell me," she finally said, "what the economic effect is expected to be?"

"Oh, I don't know that. Haven't thought about it yet."

"You have to have one. Either a calculation of economic effect or a statement that there isn't any—and we have to have a certificate of utilization. . . ."

"Well go and write one," answered Kolemasov. "You're in charge of all of that." He turned and walked over to his friends. One of them was already shuffling the dominoes on the table.

"Who wrote the application for you?" Lyubochka asked.

"Seryoga Karyaev. We thought it up together. Tell you what, try the metalworking shop, he's doing something over there now. Have a word with him."

Kolemasov sat down at the table and pulled in his dominoes.

A minute later Lyubochka was standing in the doorway of the metalworking shop, trying to spot Karyaev. She eventually saw his small, oil-smeared face with the big horn-rimmed glasses over in the corner. With a pair of pliers Karyaev was holding a long chisel against the bottom of a rusty iron boiler while another man bashed it as hard as he could with a sledgehammer. Lyubochka tried waving her notebook at them, but they were too busy to notice, so she went over herself.

"It's very simple," said Karyaev in response to Lyubochka's question. "The economic effect results from higher work rates in the metal sections. You have to figure it out."

"How?"

"As if you didn't already know. You have to figure out how much quicker operations are performed using the changeable weights, and multiply that by the number of trolley parks. Then you have to factor in the number of shears per park. And deduct the cost of the weights. I'm just giving you the general outline, okay?"

Karyaev screwed up his face at every blow of the sledge hammer, as if it was beating on his head, not the chisel, and the racket so deafened Lyubochka that she thought Karyaev was actually saying something very intelligent. Suddenly Karyaev's partner missed and slammed the sledgehammer against the boiler, and Lyubocha felt she was standing inside an immense bell for a moment. Karyaev straightened up and scratched his ear.

"Listen," he said, "I'll write you another proposal tomorrow. See that chisel? I'll weld a crossbar on to it for a handle. Then you can register it. The economic effect is calculated the same way, only you deduct the cost of the welding."

"How do I find that out?" Lyubochka asked.

"What d'you mean, how. . . . Look it up. Or phone the welding institute."

Karyaev pulled down Lyubochka by the arm. They both ducked, and some dark thing the size of a large dog whistled past over their heads.

Lyubochka straightened up, squinting at the finely membraned creature fluttering about under the ceiling, and Karyaev picked up the chisel that had fallen from the pliers, set it back in their grip, and held it against the boiler.

"Get on with it, Fyodor."

Fyodor cleared his throat and swung the sledgehammer. Lyubochka glanced at her watch and gasped in surprise: it was already ten minutes into lunch hour. She rushed over to the cafeteria.

She was too late, of course. The line already wound its way from the cash desk to the door. Lyubochka stood at the end and prepared for a wait. First she spent a while studying the mural paintings of a gigantic round loaf hovering like a UFO over a field of wheat, then she noticed the folded sheet of paper sticking out of the pocket of her padded jacket. She took it out and unfolded it.

KATMANDU: LAND OF MANY FACES, she read. Under the title the words "Instruction Manual" appeared in fine print. Lyubochka leaned against the wall and began to read:

The city of Katmandu, capital of the small state of Nepal, is situated on the picturesque foothills of the Himalayas. If the hills are viewed from the valleys below, they look like the back of a dragon lying on the ground. The ancestors of Nepal's present inhabitants therefore called this place the Dragon Hills.

The city is about three thousand years old. Katmandu is mentioned as a major cultural and religious center in many ancient chronicles. The city was known in Khan dynasty China as "Canto" and was regarded as the capital of the mythical Southern Kingdom. During the second and third centuries A.D. Buddhism reached Katmandu and quickly formed a fantastic symbiosis with the local patriarchical cults. Christianity reached the city at the same time, but failed to spread very widely among the urban upper classes and remained confined to small communities of herdsmen on the extensive lowlands to the south of the city. The local Christians are Roman Catholics, but recently the Church of Katmandu has been seeking autocephalous status.

Lyubochka heard quiet singing behind her. She turned round and saw three employees from the Economics and Planning Group standing back at the end of the line. They were wearing long sacks with holes for their heads and arms, drawn in at the waist with grey string, and thick paraffin candles were burning in their hands. The sacks were printed with some kind of figures, black umbrellas, and the inscription "USE NO HOOKS." Lyubochka went back to her reading.

At the end of the last century the Russian Dukhobor sect moved here, establishing several villages not far from the city. Their way of life painstakingly maintains certain features of a Russian 19th-century village. For instance, the walls of the huts are decorated with portraits of Emperor Alexander III and his family, cut out of the magazine Niva.

The numerous cultures and religious traditions blended within the bounds of a single city-state have transformed Katmandu into a unique architectural site. Buddhist pagodas stand side by side with Shivaite shrines, Christian churches, and synagogues. Katmandu has a higher proportion of religious buildings than most other cities in the world. However, this is not to say that the local inhabitants are excessively religious—quite the opposite, they tend to take an epicurean at-

titude to life. In Katmandu almost every day in the calendar is a holy day of some sort: some resemble European religious festivities, and members of the government or representatives of the authorities take part in these. At such times order is maintained on the streets and solemn ceremonies are performed, such as the parade of the National Guard on elephants along the main street of the city on Independence Day. The festival of the Day of Peeping Over the Edge *involves the traditional ritual use of psychotropic plants, and Katmandu temporarily assumes the appearance of a city under seige. Armored government cars patrol the streets with megaphones, calling on the silent and frightened people gathered in the squares to disperse.*

The most widespread cult in Katmandu is the sect of The Seekers of Conviction. *Its followers can often be seen on the streets of the city wearing tightly buttoned blue cassocks and carrying baskets for alms. Their spiritual practice employs intense contemplation and asceticism to achieve a realization of human life as it really is. Some of the ascetics achieve this goal, and they are known as the "convinced." They are easily recognised by the wild screams which they constantly emit. A "convinced" adept is immediately isolated in a special monastery which is called* The Nest of the Convinced, *where he spends the rest of his days, ceasing to scream only in order to take food. When they are close to death, the "convinced" begin to scream especially loudly and piercingly, and then the young adepts lead them out into the simple courtyard to die. Several of those present at this ceremony immediately become "convinced" themselves, and they are immured in rooms with cork walls, where they spend the rest of their days. They are accorded the title of* Convinced in the Nest, *which gives them the right to wear green beads. It is said that in response to a visitor's comment about how terrible it was to die among mud puddles and grunting swine, one of the "convinced" ceased his screaming for a moment and said, "Anyone who thinks that it is easier to die surrounded by your family and loved ones, lying in a comfortable bed, has no idea at all what death is."*

Katmandu is not only a cultural center with centuries-old traditions, it is also a major industrial city. Soviet specialists recently helped build an electric lamp factory here, and its products are in great demand on the world market. From ancient days the sandy beaches of Katmandu have attracted tourists from all corners of the world, and the entertainment industry here is second to none. Nepal also has a young Communist Party, which leads the struggle for better conditions for the workers of this small picturesque country.

On her small tray Lyubochka placed tomato salad, pork stew, and a glass of light Italian wine. She thought for a moment, and then put the stew back and took a scumbria with cabbage instead, paid, and went over to a corner table where the girls from the book-keeping office were waving for her to join them.

"Have you read that pamphlet?" asked Nastya Bykova, a girl with a thick layer of powder covering her unattractive face.

"Yes," Lyubochka replied as she sat down, "I read it."

"It's probably warm there," said Nastya dreamily. "Warm all year round. Lots of men. And all kinds of fruit. And we have to live here, never seeing anything. And when we die we'll probably end up no better off. Right, Olya?"

Olya thought about it, looking into her soup.

Lyubochka finished before everyone else, put the tray and the plates on the black conveyor belt, nodded to her girlfriends, and went back to the technical department.

"I'm a fool," she thought as she went upstairs. "I should have married Vaska Balalykin and gone off to the army with him. I'd be sitting somewhere in a garrison library, giving out the books. . . ."

In the corridor she bumped into Director Shushpanov just as he was coming out of a party committee meeting. She didn't even have time to feel really frightened: Shushpanov whirled around, took her by the arm, and led her along the corridor towards a poster of three gigantic faces with disgusted and wrathful expressions beneath their hard hats gazing down at a filthy little figure with a bottle protruding from his pocket.

"What are you doing right now?"

"Me? I was in the metal workshop—I'm going to do the paperwork for two rationalization proposals. But the economic—"

"Drop all that," Shushpanov whispered as if casting a spell, "and get down to the library fast. We have to get the wall newspaper done quick. There's two people down there already, you help them. All right?"

"I can't draw."

"It doesn't matter, they need things colored in. Off you go girl, like a shot!" Sushpanov spoke the last words just as though their vague coarseness was excused by the incredible happiness that had descended on Lyubochka at his proposal.

She stretched her mouth into a smile and answered: "I'm on my way! I'll just put my notebook away."

"Like a shot!" Shushpanov repeated as he walked on and swerved deftly into the men's room, leaving Lyubochka alone with the wrath and disgust of the poster at the end of the corridor.

Lyubochka turned back. Shushmanov had dragged her an extra thirty yards. She went into the technical department, put her notebook in its usual place, and changed her padded jacket for the blue workcoat hanging in the same closet. Her colleagues were crowded round the window, watching two heavenly horsemen who occasionally emerged from the low clouds. Mark Mennizinger turned to her and said:

"Lyubochka, call Vasily Balalykin."

"I already know," said Lyubochka, "thank you."

The line was busy, and five minutes later she was in the library, where the park's artist, Kostya, and the librarian, Elena Pavlovna, were leaning over two tables set together and covered with the wall newspaper, consisting of several sheets of butcher paper glued together. The pencil drawings were already finished and just had to be filled in with watercolor. Kostya handed Lyubochka a small brush with a broken handle and told her to give it a good wash in a five-gallon jar of murky water standing on the floor.

"Make sure you don't drop it in," he said in a frightened voice, "it'll sink."

She was offended by his lack of confidence in her. She washed the brush thoroughly. The part of the drawing she had to colour in was a huge curving ear of wheat. If it was real, it would have been enough to feed an entire platoon. Lyubochka began carefully applying a layer of yellow paint to it and was just beginning to feel happy about how well it was turning out, when Kostya shook her by the shoulder.

"What are you doing, eh?" he asked. "You have to bring out the third dimension. Watch me."

He dipped the brush in whitewash and began correcting what she had done. There was still no third dimension, but the ear of wheat began to look like it was cast in bronze. "Get it?"

"Yes." She put her fingers to her temples and asked, unexpectedly even to herself, "Listen what's that fairytale where they eat iron bread, do you remember?"

"Iron bread?" said Kostya in amazement, "God only knows."

Outside it was already dark and the street lamps were burning with a cold purple light. When people began coming in, the only things still to be colored in were the smiling moon and an airforce officer with a helmet that looked like a fishbowl.

Almost all the administrative staff were there, and for some reason the woman in the orange vest who wouldn't let Lyubochka into the trolley park that morning had also come. Shushpanov came up to the table, glanced at the wall newspaper, praised it, and said that there would now be a short meeting and they could go on afterwards.

Everyone took their places. Shushpanov, Shuvalov, and the woman in the orange vest made up the small presidium, and as usual the young people sat as far away as possible, beside the bookcases. The meeting began.

Shushpanov stood up, rubbed his hands together, and was

just about to say something when the door opened and Karyaev appeared, his small face smeared with oil. He was carrying the chisel with a long cross-piece welded to it. "We have to turn on the radio," he said.

Shushpanov looked at him in gloomy incomprehension, and then his face suddenly lit up.

"That's right, we have to turn on the radio," he said.

He came out from behind the table, went over to the wall, and turned the black dial of a small radio emblazoned with the Olympic emblem.

". . . *Our own correspondent in Nepal*. . . ." Background noises appeared: car horns, the wind, someone laughing in the distance.

"Standing here," a loud voice suddenly began, *"on the wide roads of modern Nepal, one is constantly amazed at the variety of nature in this astounding country. Just a few hours ago the sun was shining, there were tall palms and rosewood trees rising up to the sky, the blue cuckoos and red parrots were singing marvelously. It seemed it would go on forever, but the natural world has its own laws, and now we have moved up higher, into the thin air of the foothills. How quiet it is here! How mournfully the sky gazes down on the earth! No wonder that down below in the valleys they say that up here they eat iron bread. These mountains are certainly very harsh. But it is interesting when you come up from the valley to the deserted snowy peaks to see how many climactic zones you pass through. You notice the moment when a birch grove begins at the side of the road; further on there are rowans and lindens, and it seems that at any moment the modest houses of a plain Russian village will appear in a gap between the trees, with a pair of cows grazing behind a fence and, of course, the dome of a small log church. The next thing to come to mind is the distant ringing of a bell, and then the patterned crosses on church domes and a crowd of old women in the vestibule, bowing in obeisance and hastening to light a slim, touching candle to God. . . . One memory follows another, and soon you notice that you are not thinking about the natural world of Nepal, but about what Orthodox*

dogma calls Aerial Tribulations. Let me remind our listeners that according to traditional interpretation this is the forty days spent by souls traversing the regions inhabited by various demons who tear asunder a consciousness infected by sin. Modern science has determined that the essence of sin is the forgetting of God, and the essence of the Aerial Tribulations is endless movement along a narrowing spiral towards the point of true death. Dying is not as simple as it might seem to some people. . . . Take yourselves, for example. You believe that death is the end of everything, don't you?"

"Yes!" responded several voices in the hall. First Lyubochka heard them, and then she realized she had answered with all the rest.

"And you believe electric current cannot flow through air, don't you?"

"Yes—"

"No. You're wrong." At this point the voice had been speaking in a derisive tone for some time. *"But I have no intention of spoiling your October holiday with pointless argument, if only because you have been given an excellent opportunity to test this yourselves. My friends, you are just completing the first day of the Aerial Tribulations. In accordance with our glorious tradition, it is spent on earth."*

Someone in the hall cried out quietly. Someone else began howling. Lyubochka turned round to see who it was, then suddenly she remembered everything and howled herself. It took all her strength to keep from screaming at the top of her lungs. She had to distract herself by doing something, so she began using both hands in an attempt to scrub away the tire mark on the white blouse hanging down over her crushed chest. Everyone was obviously going through the same thing: Shushpanov was trying to plug the bullet-hole in his temple with the top of a pen, Karyaev was trying to straighten the bones of his smashed skull, Shuvalov was combing his forelock over a blue mark left by lightning, and even Kostya, obviously recalling something from a brochure on drowning, was giving himself artificial respiration.

Meanwhile the radio was declaiming:

"Oh, how touching are the attempts of souls driven by the gales of the Aerial Tribulations to convince themselves that nothing has happened! They will take the first hint that something has happened to them for some idiotic babbling on the radio! Oh, the horrors of Soviet death! What strange games people play as they die! Never having known anything but life, they take death also for life. May the balalaika orchestra conducted by Iegova Ergashev waken you in the morning. And may your day be the same as today until the moment when the pensive melody of a folk song from the Saratov Province, "O Ye Winds," drifts out over what some of you take for your collective farm, some for their submarine, some for a trolley park, and so forth. But for now let me offer you the Vologda song "Is There More Than One Path Through the Field?," following which the second day of your Aerial Tribulations will begin immediately, for there is no night here. Or rather, there is no day, but where there is no day, there is no night either. . . ."

The final words were drowned in a howling crescendo of unearthly balalaikas. The sound was so intolerable that people in the hall began screaming entirely without restraint.

Suddenly Lyubochka thought of how she might escape. Something prompted the idea that if she could get up and run into the corridor, then all this would go away. The others probably had similar ideas. Shushpanov staggered as he ran towards the window, the woman in the orange vest crawled under the table, quick-witted Karyaev reached out for the black dial of the radio, hoping something might happen if he turned it off, and Lyubochka, walking with great difficulty, hobbled towards the door. Suddenly the lights went out, and while she was feeling for the doorknob, several other people, obviously seized by the same hope, fell against her from behind. And when the door against which Lyubochka was pressed by the invisible force finally opened, it turned out that the trolley was already moving, and now she had to jump straight into a puddle.

Hermit and Six-Toes

I

"Get lost!"

"What?"

"I said, get lost. Out of my way, I'm trying to watch."

"What're you watching?"

"God, what an idiot. . . . All right, the sun."

Six-Toes lifted his gaze from the black surface of the soil, scattered with food, sawdust, and powdered peat, screwed up his eyes, and stared into the sky.

"Yeah . . . we just keep living our lives, but what's it all for? The mystery of the ages. Who has ever truly comprehended the subtle filiform essence of the lights of heaven?"

The stranger turned his head and contemplated him with an expression of curious disgust.

"Six-Toes," said Six-Toes immediately, introducing himself.

"I'm Hermit," replied the stranger. "Is that the way they talk here in your community? *Subtle filiform essence?*"

"Not my community anymore," answered Six-Toes, and then suddenly gave a whistle: "Hey, will you look at that!"

"What?" Hermit asked suspiciously.

"Look, up there! Another one's just appeared!"

"What of it?"

"That never happens in the center of the world. Three suns all at once."

Hermit sniggered condescendingly. "I've seen eleven of them at once. One at zenith and five in each epicycle. Of course, that wasn't here."

"Where was it?" asked Six-Toes.

Hermit didn't answer. He turned, walked away, and picking up a food scrap from the ground with his foot, began to eat. There was a warm, gentle wind, and two suns were reflected in the grey-green planes of the distant horizon. In this atmosphere of calm sadness Hermit became so engrossed in his thoughts that when he suddenly noticed Six-Toes standing in front of him he shuddered in surprise. "You again! Well, what do you want?"

"Nothing. I just feel like talking."

"You don't seem any too bright to me. You should get back to the community. You've wandered too far away. Go on, go back over there. . . ." He waved in the direction of a thin dirty-yellow line wriggling and trembling in the distance. It was hard to believe that was how the huge unruly crowd appeared from here.

"I would go back," said Six-Toes, "but they threw me out."

"Really? What for? Politics?"

Six-Toes nodded, scratching one leg with the other. Hermit glanced down at his feet and nodded.

"Are they real?"

"What else could they be? What they said to me was, Here we are just coming up to the Decisive Stage, and there you are with six toes on your feet. . . . Real good timing, they said. . . ."

"What 'Decisive Stage' is that?"

"I don't know. All of them milling about with long faces, especially the Twenty Closest, and I don't understand a thing. All of them running around, yelling and shouting."

"Ah," said Hermit, "I understand. No doubt it gets clearer and clearer by the hour? Gradually assuming visible shape and form?"

"That's right," said Six-Toes, astonished. "How did you know?"

"I've already seen five of these Decisive Stages. Only they all had different names."

"But how can that be?" said Six-Toes. "I know this is the first time it's happened."

"Of course it is. It would be rather interesting to see what happens the second time around. . . . But then we're talking about somewhat different things." Laughing quietly, Hermit took a few steps towards the distant community, turned his back to it, and began scraping up the ground with his feet. Very soon a cloud of sawdust, peat, and scraps of food had formed in the air behind his back. He kept glancing round, waving his arms in the air, and muttering to himself. Six-Toes felt a bit frightened.

"What were you doing?" he asked, when Hermit came back over to him, breathing heavily.

"It's a gesture," Hermit answered. "An art form. You read a poem and perform the actions to go with it."

"Which poem did you read?"

"This one," said Hermit:

"Sometimes I feel sad
Observing those I have left.
Sometimes I laugh,
And then between us
There rises up the yellow mist."

"That's not a poem," said Six-Toes. "I know all of the poems, thank God. Not by heart, of course, but I've heard all twenty-five of them. That definitely isn't one of them."

Hermit looked at him in surprise, and then seemed to understand.

"Can you remember at least one?" he asked. "Recite one for me."

"Just a moment. The twins . . . The twins . . . right,

well, to cut it short, it's about how we say one thing and we mean another. And then we say one thing and mean another again, only like the other way round. It's all very beautiful. At the end we look up at the wall and see a face that puts an end to all doubt and hesitation—"

"Enough!" Hermit interrupted.

There was silence.

Six-Toes was the first to break it: "So, did they throw you out too?"

"No, I threw all of them out."

"How could that happen?"

"All sorts of thing can happen," said Hermit. Glancing up at one of the heavenly bodies, he went on in a tone that suggested a shift from idle chatter to serious conversation: "It'll get dark soon."

"Oh, sure. Right," replied Six-Toes. "Nobody knows when it's going to get dark."

"I know. And if you want to sleep in peace, you just do what I do."

Hermit set about scraping into heaps the sawdust, peat, and various bits of garbage under his feet. Gradually a wall took shape, about the same height as himself, and enclosing a small distinct space. His construction completed, Hermit stepped back, glanced at it lovingly, and said: "There. I call it The Sanctuary of the Soul."

"Why?" asked Six-Toes."

"I like the sound of it. Are you going to build one?"

Six-Toes began scratching and scraping, but he couldn't get the hang of it. His wall kept collapsing. To tell the truth, he wasn't trying very hard, because he didn't really believe what Hermit had told him about it getting dark, so when the lights of heaven wavered and began gradually to dim, and the distant community gave out a communal gasp of horror like the wind rustling through straw, he was simultaneously overcome by two powerful feelings: the usual terror at the sudden advance of dark-

ness and an unfamiliar feeling of admiration for someone who
knew more than he did about the world.

"So be it," said Hermit. "You jump inside and I'll build another one."

"I don't know how to jump," Six-Toes answered in a quiet
voice.

"So long, then," said Hermit. Suddenly he pushed off from
the earth with all his strength, soared up into the air, and disappeared behind his wall. Then the entire structure collapsed in on
him, covering him with an even layer of sawdust and peat. The
small hillock that was formed in this way carried on shuddering
for a little while, and then a little opening appeared in its side.
Six-Toes just caught a glimpse of Hermit's eyes glittering in it
before total darkness descended.

For as long as he could remember, Six-Toes had of course
known all he needed to know about night. "It's a natural
process," some said. "We should just get on with our work," said
others, the majority. There were many shades of opinion, but the
same thing happened to everyone regardless. When the light disappeared without any apparent cause, after struggling briefly and
helplessly against the paralyzing terror, they all fell into a state of
torpor, and when they came to—when the lights began shining
again—they could remember almost nothing. When Six-Toes
was still living in the community, the same thing had happened to
him, but now, probably because his terror at the onset of night
was overlaid and doubled by his terror at being alone, the stan-
dard salvation of a coma was denied him. In the distance the community had fallen silent, but he just went on sitting there, conscious,
hunched over, beside the mound, crying quietly. He couldn't
see a thing, and when Hermit's voice suddenly pierced the darkness,
he was so frightened that he shat right there on the spot.

"Hey, stop that banging, will you?" Hermit complained. "I
can't sleep."

"I'm not banging," Six-Toes answered in a quiet voice. "It's
my heart. Talk to me for a bit, will you?"

"What about?" asked Hermit.

"Anything you like, just make it as long as you can."

"How about the nature of fear, then?"

"Oh, no, not that," squeaked Six-Toes.

"Quiet!" hissed Hermit. "Or we'll have all the rats here in a moment."

"Rats? What are they?" Six-Toes asked in cold fright.

"Creatures of the night. And of the day too, for that matter."

"Life has been cruel to me," whispered Six-Toes. "If only I had the right number of toes, I'd be sleeping with all the others. God, I'm so afraid. . . . Rats. . . ."

"Listen," said Hermit, "you keep on saying God this, God that—do they believe in God over there, then?"

"God only knows. There is something, that's for sure, but just what, nobody knows. For instance, why does it get dark? If you like you can explain it by natural causes, of course. And if you go thinking about God, you'll never get anything done in this life . . ."

"So just what can you get done in this life?"

"What a question! Why do you ask stupid questions, as if you don't know the answers already? Everyone tries as hard as he can to get to the trough. It's the law of life."

"Okay. Then what's it all for?"

"All what?"

"You know, the universe, the sky, the earth, the suns, all of it."

"What d'you mean, what for? That's just the way the world is."

"What way is it?" Hermit asked in a curious voice.

"Just the way it is. We move in space and time. According to the laws of life."

"Where to?"

"How should I know? It's the mystery of the ages. You're enough to drive anyone crazy."

"You're the one who'd drive anyone crazy. No matter what we talk about, it's all the law of life or the mystery of the ages."

"If you don't like it," said Six-Toes, offended, "then don't talk."

"I wouldn't be talking if you weren't afraid of the dark."

Six-Toes had completely forgotten about that. He focused on what he was feeling, and suddenly realized there was no fear there at all. This frightened him so much that he leapt to his feet and set off running blindly into the darkness, until his head slammed at full speed into the invisible Wall of the World.

In the distance Six-Toes could hear Hermit's cackling laughter. Placing one foot carefully in front of the other, he began making his way towards it, the only sound in the silent, impenetrable darkness that surrounded him. When he reached the mound in which Hermit was ensconced, he lay down beside it without a word and tried to ignore the cold and go to sleep. He didn't even notice when he finally did.

II

"Today we're going to climb over the Wall of the World, okay?" said Hermit.

Six-Toes was just making the approach to his sanctuary of the soul. The actual structure now turned out just like Hermit's, but he could only manage the jump by a long run up to it, and he was practising. The meaning of Hermit's words penetrated just at the moment of takeoff, with the result that he hurtled straight into the shaky construction, and the peat and sawdust, instead of settling over his body in a smooth, soft layer, ended up as an untidy heap on top of his head, while his feet stuck helplessly up into the air. Hermit helped him to scramble out and then said it again:

"Today we're going over the Wall of the World."

In the last few days Six-Toes had heard so many incredible things from Hermit that his mind was in a constant state of groaning turmoil, and his old life in the community seemed no more than an amusing fantasy—or perhaps a vulgar nightmare, he hadn't quite decided yet. But this was just too much.

Hermit carried on: "The Decisive Stage comes round after every seventy eclipses. Yesterday was the sixty-ninth. The world is ruled by numbers." He pointed to a long chain made of linked straws protruding from the earth right beside the Wall of the World.

"But how can we climb over the Wall of the World if it's the Wall of the World? The very name . . . I mean, there isn't anything on the other side. . . ."

Six-Toes was so flabbergasted by the very idea that he didn't hear a word of Hermit's dark mystical explanations, which would only have upset him even more anyway.

"So what if there isn't anything?" answered Hermit. "We should be glad of it."

"But what will we do there?"

"Live."

"What's so bad about here?"

"The fact that soon there won't be any more 'here' here, you idiot."

"Then what will there be?"

"You stay here and you'll find out soon enough. There won't be anything."

Six-Toes realized he had completely lost his bearings.

"Why are you always frightening me like this?"

"Stop whining, will you?" muttered Hermit, gazing up anxiously at some point in the sky. "Things are okay on the other side of the Wall of the World. I'd say they're a lot better than here."

He walked over to the remains of the sanctuary Six-Toes had built and began scattering them in all directions with his feet.

"What're you doing that for?" Six-Toes asked.

"Before departing from any world, you have to summarize the experience of existence there and then destroy all traces of your presence."

"Who made that up?"

"What does it matter? Okay, I did. There isn't anyone else around here to do things like that. So. . . ."

Hermit contemplated the result of his labors. The site of the collapsed structure was now perfectly smooth and quite indistinguishable from the surrounding surface of the desert.

"That's done," he said. "I've destroyed the traces. Now we have to summarize our experience. It's your turn. Climb up on that tussock and tell me about it."

Six-Toes felt like he was being tricked into doing the most difficult job, the one that was hardest to grasp, but after what happened with the eclipse he'd decided he'd better do what Hermit said. He glanced around with a shrug to make sure no one from the community had wandered over in their direction, and then clambered on to the tussock.

"What do I talk about?"

"Everything you know about the world."

"We'll be stuck here quite a while, then," said Six-Toes with a whistle.

"I doubt it," Hermit replied drily.

"All right, then. Our world. . . . This ritual of yours is plain stupid. . . ."

"Get on with it."

"Our world is a regular octagon moving at a regular speed along a linear course through space. Here we prepare ourselves for the Decisive Stage, the crowning event of our lives. At least, that's the official formula. Around the perimeter of the world runs the Wall of the World, which is the objective result of the operation of the laws of life. In the center of the world stands the combined feed-trough and drinking-trough, on which our civilization has been centered since time immemorial. The position of a member of the community relative to the troughs is determined by his social standing and his merits—"

"I've not heard that part before," Hermit interrupted. "What are these merits, and what's social standing?"

"Well. . . . How can I explain it? It's when someone actually reaches the trough."

"And who does reach it?"

"I told you, the ones who have the greatest merits. Or the highest social standing. Take me, for instance, I used to have kind of average merits, but now I don't have any. You mean to say you don't know the popular model of the universe?"

"No, I don't," said Hermit.

"Oh, come on. . . . So how come you were preparing for the Decisive Stage?"

"I'll tell you later. Carry on."

"That's almost all there is. What else is there? Beyond the province of the community lies the great desert, and everything ends in the Wall of the World. Turncoats like us take refuge by the wall."

"Turncoats. Okay. So which way round should the coat be? Where's the tailor?"

"There you go again. . . . Not even the Twenty Closest can tell you that. It's the mystery of the ages."

"Okay, then. So what's the mystery of the ages?"

"The law of life," Six-Toes answered, trying to keep his voice down. Something in Hermit's tone of voice made him feel uneasy.

"All right. And what's the law of life?"

"It's the mystery of the ages."

"The *mystery* of the ages," Hermit repeated in a strange, thin voice, and he began slowly circling towards Six-Toes.

"You stop that!" Six-Toes shouted from fear. "You and your ritual!"

But Hermit had already gotten a grip on himself.

"Okay," he said. "Get down."

Six-Toes climbed down from the tussock, and Hermit clambered up to take his place, wearing an expression of serious concentration. For a while he said nothing, as though listening carefully to something, then he raised his head and began.

"I came here from another world," he said, "in the days when you were still very small. I came to that other world from a third world, and so on. I have been in five worlds in all. They are all just like this one, with almost nothing to distinguish them from each other. The universe in which we find ourselves consists of an immense enclosed space. In the language of the gods it is known as 'the Lunacharsky Broiler Combine,' but what that means even they do not know."

"You know the language of the gods?" Six-Toes asked in amazement.

"A little. Don't interrupt. There are seventy worlds altogether in the universe. We are in one of them at the moment. These worlds are fastened to an endless black belt which moves slowly in a circle. Above it, on the surface of the sky, there are hundreds of identical suns. They do not move over us, it is we who move below them. Try to picture it."

Six-Toes closed his eyes, a strained expression dawning on his face.

"No, I can't," he said eventually.

"Okay," said Hermit. "Listen. All of the seventy worlds in the universe are together known as the Chain of Worlds. At least, they can be called that. In each of the worlds there is life, but it does not exist continuously, it appears and disappears in cycles. The Decisive Stage occurs in the center of the universe, through which all of the worlds pass in turn. In the language of the gods it is known as Shop Number One. At the moment our world is located at its very threshold. When the Decisive Stage is concluded and the world emerges renewed from the far side of Shop Number One, everything starts all over again. Life appears, runs through its cycle and at the appointed time it is plunged back into Shop Number One."

"How do you know all this?" Six-Toes asked in a half-whisper.

"I've traveled around a lot," said Hermit, "and picked up the secret knowledge crumb by crumb. In one world they knew one thing, in another something else."

"Maybe you know where we come from?"

"Yes, I do. But what do they say about that in your world?"

"They say it's an objective given—the law of life."

"I see. You're asking me about one of the most profound mysteries of the universe and I'm not even sure I can trust you with it. But since there isn't anyone else around, I suppose I'll tell you anyway. We appear in this world out of white spheres. They're not actually spheres, they're slightly elongated, and one end is narrower than the other, but that's not important right now."

"Spheres. White spheres," repeated Six-Toes, and then he suddenly keeled over and his body hit the ground. The burden of what he had learnt descended on him like a physical weight, and for a second he thought he was going to die. Hermit jumped down and began to shake him with all his might. Six-Toes gradually regained some clarity of mind.

"What's wrong with you?" Hermit asked, alarmed.

"Oh, I remembered. That's how it was. We used to be white spheres lying on long shelves in a place that was very warm and damp. And then from inside we began breaking open the spheres and . . . our world came up from somewhere below us, and then we were already in it. . . . But why doesn't anyone remember all this?"

"There are worlds in which they remember," said Hermit. "It's only the fifth and sixth prenatal matrix. Not really all that deep, and only one part of the truth. But even so they isolate the ones who remember it, so they won't interfere with the preparations for the Decisive Stage, or whatever it happens to be called. It has a different name in every world. In my world, for instance, it was known as the Completion of Construction, although no one there ever built anything at all."

Clearly overcome by sadness at the memory of his own world, Hermit fell silent.

"Listen," Six-Toes said after a little while, "where do the white spheres come from?"

Hermit looked at him approvingly.

"Before I was ready to ask that question," he said, "I needed much more time. But this is where things get much more complicated. One ancient legend says that these eggs appear from within us, but that could just be a metaphor. . . ."

"From within us? I don't understand. Where did you hear that?"

"I made it up myself. Where could you hear anything around here?" Hermit said in a voice that suddenly sounded weary.

"But you said it was an ancient legend."

"That's right. I made it up as an ancient legend."

"What d'you mean? What for?"

"You see, an ancient sage, you could call him a prophet"— this time Six-Toes guessed who was meant—"once said that what matters is not what is said, but who says it. Part of the meaning I was trying to express is that my words fulfil the function of an ancient legend. But how can you be expected. . . ." Hermit glanced up at the sky and interrupted his own train of thought: "Enough of that. It's time to go."

"Go where?"

"To the community."

Six-Toes gawped at him. "We were going to climb over the Wall of the World. What do we need the community for?"

"Don't you have any idea what the community really is?" Hermit asked. "It is precisely a device for climbing over the Wall of the World."

III

Although there was not a single object you could hide behind in the desert, Six-Toes crept along furtively, and the closer they came to the community, the more obviously criminal his stride became. Gradually the huge crowd, which from a distance had seemed like a single wriggling creature, disintegrated into individual bodies; they could even make out scowls of astonishment on the faces which had noticed them approaching.

"The main thing," Hermit whispered, repeating his final instruction, "is to be insolent, but not too insolent. We have to make them mad, but not so mad that they tear us to pieces. Just keep an eye on what I do."

"Hey, Six-Toes is back!" someone ahead of them shouted cheerfully. "You old bastard! Hey, Six-Toes, who's that with you?"

For some strange reason at the sound of this muddle-headed abuse Six-Toes was overwhelmed by nostalgic childhood memories. Hermit, walking right behind him, seemed to sense this, and he poked Six-Toes in the back. The individuals on the very edge of the community were quite widely separated. This was where the cripples and the contemplatives lived, the ones who did not like to be crowded, and it was easy to make your way past them. But the further they went, the denser the crowd became, and very soon Hermit and Six-Toes found themselves in an unbearable crush. It was still possible to move forward, but only at the cost of squabbling with your neighbors, and by the time that the trembling roof of the troughs had appeared above the heads of the crowd in front of them, it was impossible to take another step forward.

"It never ceases to amaze me," Hermit said quietly to Six-Toes, "just how wisely everything is arranged here. Those who stand closest to the troughs are happy, mostly because they are constantly thinking about the others who want to take their place. And those who wait all their lives for a narrow crack to appear between the bodies up in front are happy because they have something to hope for. That is harmony and unity."

"Anything wrong with that?" asked a voice from one side.

"Yes, I don't like it," answered Hermit.

"And just what is it that you don't like?"

"All of it." Hermit made a sweeping gesture which took in the crowd, the majestic dome of the troughs, the glittering yellow light in the sky and, away in the distance, the barely visible Wall of the World.

"I see. So where is it any better?"

"Nowhere, that's what's so tragic!" Hermit screamed in a martyred voice. "That's the whole problem! If there was anywhere better, why would I waste my time here, discussing life with you?"

"And does your comrade share these views?" asked the voice. "Why is he staring at the ground?"

Six-Toes looked up—he had been gazing down at his feet, because that way he could keep his involvement in what was happening to the minimum—and saw the owner of the voice. He had a fat, flabby face, and when he spoke the anatomical details of his larynx were clearly visible. Six-Toes immediately realized that he was facing one of the Twenty Closest, the living conscience of the era.

"The reason you're so miserable, my young friends," he said, in an unexpectedly friendly tone, "is that you're not preparing for the Decisive Stage along with everybody else. If you were, you wouldn't have time for such thoughts. Even I sometimes have such thoughts. . . . You know, our only salvation lies in work." Then, in exactly the same tone he concluded: "Take them."

There was a movement in the crowd, and Hermit and Six-Toes immediately found themselves hemmed in tightly on all sides.

"We don't give a damn about you," Hermit said in an equally friendly voice. "Where are you going to take us? You have nowhere to take us. All you can do is banish us again. In the words of the old proverb, 'You can't just toss it over the Wall of the World'."

At this point an expression of confused anxiety appeared on Hermit's face, the flabby-faced individual raised his eyebrows, and their eyes met.

"Now there's an interesting idea. We haven't tried that before. The proverb does exist, of course, but the will of the people is stronger."

He was clearly exhilarated by the idea. He turned away and started giving orders.

"Attention! Everybody into line! We're going to do something we hadn't planned on."

It didn't take very long from the moment Flabby-Face issued his order to line up the procession for approaching the Wall of the World and lead Hermit and Six-Toes along at its center.

The procession was impressive. The flabby-faced individual walked at its head, followed by two specially appointed Old Mothers (nobody, including Flabby-Face, knew what their title meant—it was just a tradition), who shouted abuse at Hermit and Six-Toes through their tears, mourning and cursing them at the same time. Next came the two criminals themselves, and bringing up the rear was the common crowd.

"And so," said Flabby-Face, once the procession had stopped, "the fearful moment of retribution is upon us. I am sure, my friends, that we shall all be fighting back our tears when these two turncoats vanish into nonexistence, won't we? And may this alarming event serve as a terrible warning to all of us, to the whole community. . . . Sob louder, Mothers!"

The Old Mothers fell down to the ground and burst into such mournful wailing that many of those present turned away and began swallowing hard. From time to time, however, the Mothers would leap up with eyes blazing from their squirming in the tear-spattered dust and hurl the most terrible and irrefutable accusations at Hermit and Six-Toes, before they collapsed again.

"So, have you repented?" Flabby-Face asked after a little while, "Have the Mothers' tears not roused your sense of shame?"

"I should think so," Hermit answered, shifting his keen gaze from the ceremony to the heavenly bodies and then back again. "How do you intend to throw us over?"

The flabby-faced individual pondered the question. The Old

Mothers fell silent too, then one of them got up out of the dust, shook herself off, and said: "Maybe a ramp?"

"A ramp," said Hermit. "That would take five eclipses. And we are impatient to conceal our unmasked shame in the void."

The flabby-faced individual screwed up his eyes, glanced at Hermit, and nodded approvingly.

"They understand," he said to one of his own people, "they're just pretending. Ask them if they have anything to suggest themselves."

A few minutes later a living pyramid reached up almost to the very top of the Wall of the World. The ones on the top screwed up their eyes and hid their faces in order not to glance out there, at the end of everything.

"Up!" someone shouted at Hermit and Six-Toes, and they started climbing up the precarious rows of shoulders and backs, supporting each other as they made their way towards the top of the wall lost in the distance above their heads.

From the top they could see the entire silent community, carefully watching what was happening from a distance, and could make out certain details of the sky that had not been visible before. They noticed the thick hose that descended out of infinity into the troughs—it didn't look as magnificent from up here as it did from the ground. Leaping up lightly onto the top of the Wall of the World as though onto a mere tussock, Hermit helped Six-Toes to take a seat beside him and shouted down: "Everything's in order!"

At the sound of his shout someone in the pyramid lost his balance; it swayed a few times and then collapsed. Everyone in it went tumbling down to the foot of the wall.

Clutching the cold sheet metal, Six-Toes gazed down at the tiny faces looking up to him, and at the cheerless grey-brown expanses of his homeland. He gazed at the corner of his homeland where there was a large green spot on the Wall of the World, where he had spent his childhood. "I'll never see any of this

again," he thought, and even though he wished he wouldn't, he
felt a lump rise in his throat. He pressed against his side a small
piece of earth with a straw stuck in it, and pondered how rapidly
and inexorably everything in his life was changing.

"Goodbye, our sons!" the Old Mothers shouted up from
below, first bowing down to the earth and then sobbing as they
threw heavy pieces of peat up at them.

Hermit raised himself up on tiptoe and shouted loudly:

> *"I always knew*
> *That I would quit*
> *This heartless world—"*

At this point, he was struck by a large piece of peat, and he
tumbled backwards off the wall. Six-Toes cast a final glance
below over everything that he was leaving behind, and noticed
someone waving to him from the distant crowd. He waved back.
Then, closing his eyes tightly, he took a step backwards.

For a few seconds he tumbled untidily through empty space,
then with a sudden painful impact he landed on something hard
and opened his eyes. He was lying on a black shiny surface of
some unfamiliar material. Rising up above him was the Wall of
the World, looking just the same as it had on the other side, and
beside him, his arm extended towards the wall, stood Hermit. He
was completing his recitation of the poem:

> *"—But that it would be thus*
> *I had no inkling. . . ."*

IV

Now that they were walking along the gigantic black belt, Six-
Toes could see that Hermit had told him the truth. The belt and
the world they had just left really were moving slowly in relation
to other cosmic objects fixed in space (the nature of which Six-

Toes could not understand), and the suns were motionless—once you stepped off the black belt it was all quite clear.

The world they had left was now slowly being drawn towards a pair of green steel gates which the belt ran under. Hermit said that was the entrance to Shop Number One. Strangely enough, Six-Toes was not in the least overawed by the magnificence of the objects filling the universe; in fact he felt a certain mild irritation. "Is that all there is?" he thought, vaguely disgusted. In the distance he could see two worlds like the one that they had just left. They were also moving along on the black belt and from where he stood they looked rather squalid. At first Six-Toes thought he and Hermit were on their way to another world, but when they were halfway there, Hermit told him to jump from the motionless border of the moving belt along which they were walking down into a dark, bottomless crevice.

"It's soft," he said to Six-Toes, but Six-Toes took a step backwards, shaking his head. Without another word, Hermit jumped himself, and there was nothing left for Six-Toes but to leap after him.

This time he almost broke something on the hard, cold surface of large brown slabs of stone. The slabs extended off as far as the horizon, and for the first time in his life Six-Toes understood the meaning of the word "infinity."

"What is it?" Six-Toes asked.

"Tiles," Hermit answered him with a meaningless word, and then changed the subject. "The night will begin soon, and we have to get all the way across there. We'll have to go part of the way in darkness."

Hermit seemed seriously concerned about something. Gazing off into the distance Six-Toes was able to make out some yellow cube-shaped rocks—Hermit told him they were called "boxes." There were plenty of them, and the spaces between them he could see were strewn with light-colored wood shavings. From the distance it all looked like a scene from some dimly remembered childhood dream.

"Let's go," said Hermit, setting off briskly.

"Tell me," said Six-Toes, slipping on the tiled surface as he walked beside him, "how do you know when the night's about to start?"

"From the clock," Hermit answered. "It's one of the heavenly bodies. At present it's up above us on the right, that disc with the black zigzags on it."

Six-Toes looked up at the familiar detail of the vault of heaven, to which he had never previously paid any particular attention.

"When some of those black lines reach a certain position, which I'll tell you about later, the light goes out," said Hermit. "It's going to happen any second now. Count to ten."

"One, two—" Six-Toes began, and suddenly it was dark.

"Don't fall behind," said Hermit, "or you'll get lost."

He needn't have said it, since Six-Toes was almost treading on his heels. The only remaining source of light in the universe was the yellow beam that slanted from behind the green gates of Shop Number One. The place towards which Hermit and Six-Toes were heading was quite close to the gates, but Hermit assured him that it was the safest.

All they could see now was a distant strip of yellow under the gates and a few tiles around them. Six-Toes fell into a strange state, feeling as though the darkness was crushing in on them in the same way that the crowd had squeezed them only a while before. There was danger on every side, and Six-Toes sensed it acutely like a cold draft blowing from all sides at once. When his fear became too strong for him to go on, he raised his gaze from the tiles to the strip of yellow light under the gates and then remembered the community, which had looked almost like the same from a distance. He felt as though they were walking into a kingdom inhabited by fire-spirits, and he was just about to tell Hermit about it, when Hermit suddenly stopped and raised his arm.

"Quiet," he said. "Rats. Over to our right."

There was nowhere to run. The expanse of tiles extended into the distance on every side, and the strip of light was still too far ahead. Hermit turned to the right and stood in a strange pose, telling Six-Toes to hide behind him. Six-Toes did so only too willingly, and with quite remarkable speed.

At first he couldn't make out anything at all, and then in the darkness he sensed, rather than saw, the rapid movement of a large, agile body. It halted precisely at the limit of his vision.

"It's waiting," Hermit said softly, "for us to go on. We only have to take a single step, and it will fling itself at us."

"Aha, I'll fling myself, all right" said the rat, emerging from the darkness. "Like a bundle of malice and fury. Like a creature truly begotten of the night."

"Oh," Hermit gasped, "One-Eye. And I thought we'd really had it. Let me introduce you."

Six-Toes stared suspiciously into the intelligent conical face with the long moustaches and two round black beads for eyes.

"One-Eye," said the rat in self-introduction and waved his indecently naked tail.

"Six-Toes," said Six-Toes in reply, and asked: "Why do they call you One-Eye, when you have two perfectly good eyes?"

"That's because my third eye has been opened," One-Eye answered, "and I've only one third eye. In a certain sense anyone whose third eye is open is one-eyed."

"What's a—" Six-Toes began, but Hermit cut him off before he could finish.

"Why don't we take a stroll," he suggested gallantly, "over to those boxes? The night road is wearisome without a companion to talk to."

Six-Toes was deeply offended.

"By all means," One-Eye agreed, turning his back on Six-Toes (who was now presented with his first clear view of the huge muscular body), and stepping out beside Hermit, who had to walk very fast to keep up with him. Six-Toes ran along behind, looking at One-Eye's feet and the muscles rippling under his skin, worrying how this encounter might have ended had One-Eye not been an acquaintance of Hermit's, and trying very hard not to tread on the rat's tail. Their conversation rapidly began to sound like the continuation of a previous discussion; they were obviously old friends.

"Freedom! My God, what's that?" One-Eye asked, laughing. "Is that running around the combine, confused and alone, after you've just dodged the knife again for the tenth time, or the hundredth? Is that what freedom is?"

"There you go substituting one thing for another again," answered Hermit. "That's nothing but the search for freedom. I shall never accept that infernal picture—the world you believe in. It's all because you feel like an alien in this universe that was created for us."

"The rats may believe it was created for us—I don't say that because I agree with them. You're right, of course, but not completely right—and not about the most important thing. You say this universe was created for you? No, it was created because of you, but not for you. Do you understand?"

Hermit lowered his head and walked on in silence.

"All right then," said One-Eye, "it's time for me to say goodbye. I was expecting you to turn up a bit later, but we've met anyway. I'm going away tomorrow."

"Where to?"

"Beyond the bounds of everything that can be spoken of. One of the old burrows led me to an empty concrete pipe that runs so far I couldn't even imagine how long it is. I met some rats there, and they say that the pipe goes on deeper and deeper, until it emerges into another universe down below us. There are only male gods and they all wear the same green clothing. They perform complicated rituals around immense idols which stand in gigantic shafts."

One-Eye slowed his pace.

"I turn right here," he said. "They say the food there is indescribable. And this entire universe would fit into one single shaft down there. Why don't you come along with me?"

"No," replied Hermit, "our way does not lie downwards."

For the first time since the conversation began, he seemed to recall the existence of Six-Toes.

"In that case," said One-Eye, "I wish you success on your journey, wherever it may take you. Farewell."

One-Eye nodded to Six-Toes and disappeared into the darkness as suddenly as he had emerged.

Hermit and Six-Toes walked the rest of the way in silence. As they came closer to the boxes, they had to pick their way across all the heaps of shavings. At long last they reached their goal, a declivity in the shavings with a heap of soft rags lying in it, gently illuminated by the light from beneath the gates of Shop Number One. Close by the wall stood a huge ribbed structure which Hermit said had once emitted such intense heat that he couldn't even approach it. He was rummaging about in the rags to make himself comfortable for the night, and Six-Toes decided not to pester him with questions, especially since he felt sleepy himself. He burrowed into the rags and fell into oblivion.

He was woken by a distant scraping, the sound of steel grinding on wood, and screams of such utter hopelessness that he rushed over to Hermit immediately: "What is that?"

"Your world's passing through its Decisive Stage," Hermit answered.

"What?"

"Death has come," Hermit said simply. He turned away, pulled a scrap of rag over himself, and fell asleep.

V

When he woke, Hermit glanced over at Six-Toes trembling in the corner, his eyes red from crying, then cleared his throat and began rummaging in the rags. Soon he had taken out ten identical iron objects that looked like sections cut from a thick six-sided pipe.

"Take a look at these," he said to Six-Toes.

"What are they?" Six-Toes asked.

"The gods call them nuts."

Six-Toes seemed on the point of asking another question, but instead he waved his hand in the air and burst into tears again.

"What in the world's the matter?" asked Hermit.

"They're all dead," Six-Toes babbled. "Every last one of them—"

"What of it?" said Hermit. "You'll die too. And you can be sure you'll be dead for just as long as they will."

"Yes, but I feel sorry for them."

"Sorry for who? The Old Mothers?

"Remember how they threw us over the wall?" Six-Toes asked. "When everybody was ordered to keep his eyes shut? I waved to them, and somebody waved back, and when I think that he's dead too. . . . And whatever made him do that has died with him. . . ."

"Yes," said Hermit, "that really is very sad."

There was silence, broken only by the mechanical sounds behind the green gates through which Six-Toes' former home had glided.

"Tell me," Six-Toes asked, his voice hoarse from crying, "what happens after we die?"

"It's hard to say," answered Hermit. "I've had many visions about it, but I don't know how much I can trust them."

"Tell me about them, will you?"

"As a rule, after death we are plunged into Hell. I've counted at least fifty variations on what happens. Sometimes the dead are divided up and cooked in immense frying pans. Sometimes they are roasted whole in an iron-walled room with a glass door where there are roaring blue flames or white-hot metal pillars radiating intense heat. Sometimes we are boiled in huge vessels of various colors, and, sometimes, quite the opposite, we are frozen in a lump of ice. All in all, not a very comforting prospect."

"But who does all that?"

"Who? The gods, of course."

"But why?"

"That's simple, we happen to be their food."

Six-Toes shuddered and then stared down intently at his own trembling knees.

"They like the legs best of all," Hermit observed. "And the arms too. It's your arms I wanted to talk to you about. Hold them out."

Six-Toes held out his arms in front of him: skinny and powerless, they were a pitiful sight.

"There was a time when we used them to fly," said Hermit, "but then everything changed."

"What does 'to fly' mean?"

"Nobody knows exactly. The only thing we do know is that you need strong arms for it. A lot stronger than yours or even mine. What I want to do now is teach you an exercise to do. Get two of the nuts."

Six-Toes struggled to drag over two of the stupendously heavy objects to Hermit's feet.

"Right. Now stick the ends of your arms into the holes."

Six-Toes did that too.

"Now lift the nuts up and down, up and down. . . . That's right."

After a minute of this Six-Toes was so exhausted he couldn't keep lifting the nuts no matter how hard he tried.

"I can't," he said, dropping his arms so the nuts crashed down on to the floor.

"Now watch how I do it," said Hermit, putting five nuts on the end of each arm. He held his arms out to the side for several minutes and didn't seem to get tired at all.

"How about that?"

"That's fantastic," sighed Six-Toes, "but why are you just holding them still?"

"With this exercise there's a difficulty that arises at a certain point. Later on you'll understand what I mean."

"Are you sure you can learn to fly this way?"

"No, I'm not sure. On the contrary, I suspect it's quite pointless."

"Then what's it good for? If you know yourself that it's quite pointless?"

"How can I put it? I know all sorts of other things apart from this, and one of them is that if you're in the dark and you glimpse even the slightest glimmering of light, you have to move towards it. You don't stop to ponder whether there's any point to it. Maybe there really isn't any point. But there's certainly no point in just sitting there in the dark. Do you understand?"

Six-Toes didn't answer.

"We only stay alive as long as we have hope," said Hermit. "And if you lose hope, you mustn't ever let yourself realize it. Then something just might change. But you should never seriously rely on that."

Six-Toes was exasperated: "That's all wonderful, but what does it really mean?"

"What it really means for you is that every day you're going to exercise with these nuts until you can do what I do."

"Is that the only thing I can do?"

"There are alternatives; for instance, you can prepare for the Decisive Stage. But you'll have to do that on your own."

VI

"Listen, Hermit, you know everything there is to know. Tell me what love is."

"Strange, where did you hear that word?"

"When they drove me out of the community, they asked

me if I loved the things that should be loved. I said I didn't know."

"I doubt if I can explain it to you. You can only learn by example. Imagine you've fallen into water and you're drowning. Can you imagine that?"

"Uhu!"

"And now imagine that just for a second you're able to lift your head above water, see the light, take a gulp of air, and feel your hands touch something, so you grab hold and cling to it. So, if you can imagine that all of your life you are drowning—and that's certainly nothing but the truth—then love is what helps you keep your head above water."

"Do you mean love for the things that should be loved?"

"That's not important. Although, generally speaking, you can love the things that should be loved even when you've gone under. It can be anything at all. What does it matter what you grab hold of, as long as it keeps you afloat? The worst thing is if it turns out to be someone else—he can always pull his hand away. If you want to keep it simple, love is the reason why everyone is where they are. Except maybe the dead . . . although—"

"I don't think I've ever loved anyone," Six-Toes broke in.

"No, it's happened to you too. Remember how you sat there crying your eyes out, thinking about the person who waved back to you when they were throwing us over the wall? That was love. You don't know why he did it. Maybe he just thought he was mocking you a bit more subtly than all the rest—that's probably what it was. That means you behaved very stupidly, but absolutely correctly. Love gives meaning to what we do, even though it actually has no meaning."

"So you mean that love deceives us? Is it something like a dream?"

"No. Love is something like love, and a dream is a dream. Everything that you do, you do out of nothing but love. Otherwise you would just sit on the ground and howl in terror. Or in disgust."

"But the reason lots of people do what they do has nothing to do with love."

"Nonsense. Those people don't do anything at all."

"Is there anything you love, Hermit?"

"Yes."

"What is it?"

"I don't know. Something that comes to me sometimes. Sometimes it's some kind of thought, sometimes the nuts, sometimes a dream. The important thing is that I always recognize it, whatever form it takes, and I greet it as best I can."

"How?"

"By becoming calm."

"Does that mean you're worried all the rest of the time?"

"No, I'm always calm. It's just that this calm is the very best thing I have in me, and when this thing I love comes to me, I offer it my calmness."

"And what do you think is best about me?"

"About you? Probably when you sit there quietly somewhere in a corner."

"Really?"

"I don't know. If you really want to, you can work out what the best thing in you is by thinking what it is you offer when you feel love. What did you feel, when you were thinking about the person who waved to you?"

"Sadness."

"Well, that means the best thing in you is your sadness, and that's how you'll always greet anything you love."

Hermit glanced round and listened to something.

"Do you want to take a look at the gods?" he asked suddenly.

"Not right now, please," Six-Toes answered in panic.

"Don't be afraid. They're very stupid—not at all frightening. Just take a look. There they are, over there."

Two vast beings were walking quickly along the path by the conveyor belt, their figures so huge that their heads were lost in the semi-darkness under the ceiling. Walking behind them came

another similar form, only shorter and fatter, carrying a vessel in
the shape of a truncated cone, with the narrow end towards the
ground. The first two stopped not far from where Hermit and
Six-Toes were sitting and began making low growling sounds—
Six-Toes guessed that they were talking—and the third being
went over to the wall, set the vessel on the floor, plunged a pole
with bristles on it into the vessel and then moved it across the
dirty-grey wall, leaving a fresh dirty-grey line. There was a
strange smell.

"Listen," Six-Toes said in a scarcely audible whisper, "you
said you know their language. What are they saying?"

"These two? Just a second. The first is saying, 'I want a skin-
ful.' And the other's saying, 'You just keep away from Masha
from now on'."

"What's a Masha?"

"It's a region of the world."

"Ah. . . . And what does the first one want to fill his skin
with?"

"Masha, probably," Hermit replied after a pause for thought.

"But how can he fit a whole part of the world inside him?"

"Well, they are gods, after all."

"And what's that one, the fat one, saying?"

"She's not saying anything, she's singing. About how when
she dies she wants to become a willow tree. Actually, that's my favorite song of the gods—it's a pity I don't know what a willow
tree is."

"Do the gods die, then?"

"Sure they do. That's what they're busy with most of the
time."

The two tall beings walked on. "How magnificent!" Six-Toes
thought in awe. The heavy footfalls of the gods and their low
voices died away and there was silence. A draft swirled the dust
along above the tiled surface of the floor and Six-Toes felt as
though he was looking down from some unimaginably high
mountain at an expanse of strange rocky desert where the same

things happen again and again for millions and milions of years:
the wind rushes over the surface of the land, bearing along the
remnants of lives that once belonged to somebody, and from a
distance they look just like pieces of straw, scraps of paper, or
woodshavings. "There'll come a time," Six-Toes thought, "when
someone else will look down from here and think about me, without even knowing that he is thinking about me. Just as I'm thinking about someone who felt the same as me, but God only knows
when that was. In every day there is a point which binds it to the
past and the future. What a sad place this world is. . . ."

"And yet there is something in it that justifies even the very
saddest life," Hermit said suddenly.

"To die and be a willow tree," the fat goddess was crooning
softly beside her bucket of paint. Six-Toes lowered his head onto
his arm in sadness, but Hermit remained absolutely calm, staring
off into the emptiness, as though he was gazing over thousands of
invisible heads.

VII

While Six-Toes spent his time exercising with the nuts, dozens of
worlds departed into Shop Number One. There were creaking
and banging sounds behind the green gates as something happened there, and Six-Toes broke into a cold sweat and began
trembling at the thought of what it might be, but this lent him
strength. His arms had grown noticeably longer and stronger,
and now they were just like Hermit's, but so far there had been
no other result. The only thing Hermit knew was that you used
your arms to fly, but what "flying" meant wasn't clear. Hermit
believed it was some special method of instantaneous displace-
ment in space: you had to imagine the place you wanted to get to,
and then mentally command your arms to take your entire body
there. He spent days in meditation, trying to move himself just a
few steps, but nothing came of it.

"Probably," he said to Six-Toes, "our arms are not strong enough yet. We'll just have to carry on exercising."

One day, when Hermit and Six-Toes, seated on their bundle of rags among the boxes, were contemplating the essence of things, something very unpleasant happened. Darkness suddenly fell, and when Six-Toes opened his eyes he saw the unshaven face of one of the gods suspended in space in front of him.

"Well, just look where they've got to!" said the face, and then a pair of immense dirty hands seized Hermit and Six-Toes, dragged them out from behind the boxes, carried them with unbelievable speed across the immense space, and threw them into one of the worlds that was already close to Shop Number One. At first Hermit and Six-Toes took this all calmly, even with a certain irony. They settled in beside the Wall of the World and began making their soul-sanctuaries, but then the god unexpectedly came back, dragged Six-Toes out, and looked him over carefully, smacking his lips in amazement. Then he tied a piece of sticky blue ribbon round his leg and threw him back. A few minutes later several of the gods arrived together. They lifted Six-Toes out and took turns looking at him with delighted expressions on their faces.

"I don't like this," said Hermit, when the gods finally went away. "It looks bad."

"I think so too," said Six-Toes, scared out of his wits. "Maybe I should take this crap off?"

He pointed to the blue ribbon wrapped around his leg.

"Better not take it off just yet," said Hermit.

For a while there was gloomy silence, then Six-Toes said: "It's all because of my six toes. Let's get out of here fast, they'll be looking for us again. They know about the boxes, but there must somewhere else we can hide?"

Hermit became even more morose, and instead of answering the question, he suggested they take a walk to the local community to unwind. But as it happened, an entire deputation was already making its way towards them from the distant twin-troughs. Judging from the fact that when they were still twenty paces away from them, the members of the delegation fell to the ground and began crawling, their intentions had to be serious. Hermit ordered Six-Toes to retreat, while he went ahead to find out what was the matter. When he came back, he said:

"I've really never seen anything like this before. They're obviously very pious. At least, they saw you associating with the gods and now they think you're the Messiah and I'm your disciple, or something like that."

"So what's going to happen now? What do they want?"

"They want us to visit them. They say some path or other has been made straight, something or other has been bound fast, and other things like that. And most important of all, it's exactly what they have in their scriptures. I don't understand a thing, but I think we should probably go along."

"Let's go, then," said Six-Toes with an indifferent shrug of his shoulders. He felt dark presentiments.

On the way it cost Hermit a lot of effort to rebuff their repeated and persistent attempts to carry him on their shoulders. Nobody dared so much as lift their eyes to Six-Toes, much less approach him, and he walked along at the center of a large circle of emptiness.

When they arrived they seated Six-Toes on a tall pile of straw, while Hermit remained at its foot and fell into conversation with the local spiritual authorities, about twenty of them, easily distinguished by their fat, flabby faces. He blessed them and clambered up the heap of straw to Six-Toes, who was now in such a bad mental state that he didn't even respond to Hermit's ritual bow, but everybody found that entirely natural anyway.

It turned out that they'd all been expecting the advent of the Messiah for a long time, because the approach of the Decisive Stage—which was called the Day of Condiment here, a clear indication that the local inhabitants had moments of serious insight—had been exercising their minds for ages, while the local spiritual authorities had become so gorged and idle that they answered every question put to them with a brief gesture of the head in the direction of the ceiling. And so the appearance of Six-Toes and his disciple had proved very timely indeed.

"They're waiting for a sermon," said Hermit.

"Well, spin them some kind of story, then," Six-Toes blurted out. "You know perfectly well I'm just plain stupid."

At the word stupid, his voice trembled, and it was clear to everyone that he was on the verge of tears.

"They're going to eat me, those gods," he said, "I can feel it."

"Come on, calm down," said Hermit. He turned to the crowd around the heap of straw and adopted a prayerful posture, turning his face to the heavens and raising his arms on high. "All of you below!" he shouted. "Soon you shall enter Hell. There all shall be roasted and the most sinful among you shall first be marinated in vinegar!"

A gasp of horror ran though the air above the crowd.

"But I, by the will of the gods and their emissary, my master, wish to teach you how to save yourselves. To do this you must conquer sin—but do you even know what sin is?"

The only answer was silence.

"Sin is excess weight. Your flesh is sinful, for because of it the gods strike you down. Why, do you think, the Decisive Stage . . . the Day of Judgment is fast approaching? It is because you are growing fat. For the thin shall be saved, but the fat shall not. Verily I say unto you: not a single bony and blue one shall be cast into the fire, but the fat and the pink shall all be there. But those who from this day forth until the very Day of Judgment shall fast, shall be born again. Oh, Lord! And now arise and sin no more!"

But no one stood up, they all lay there on the ground, staring in silence, some at Hermit waving his hands, some at the gulf of the ceiling above them. Many wept. The only ones who didn't seem impressed by Hermit's speech were the high priests.

"Why did you say that?" Six-Toes whispered when Hermit lowered himself on to the straw beside him. "They believed you!"

"Well, was I lying?" answered Hermit. "If they lose a lot of weight, they'll be sent on a second feeding cycle, and then maybe on a third. We can't waste any more time on them, let's think about our own business."

VIII

Hermit spoke frequently with the community, teaching them how to make themselves appear as unappetizing as possible, and Six-Toes spent most of his time sitting on his mountain of straw and contemplating the nature of flight. He took almost no part in the discussions and only occasionally bestowed on the laymen who crept closer to him an absent-minded blessing. The former high priests, who had not the slightest intention of going hungry, gazed at him with hatred in their eyes, but there was nothing they could do, because different gods kept coming to their world, grabbing Six-Toes, looking at him closely and showing him to one another. On one occasion the world was even visited by a heavy-jowled old god with grey hair surrounded by a large retinue, to whom the other gods showed the utmost deference. When the old god picked him up, Six-Toes deliberately shat straight onto his cold trembling palm, after which he was rather roughly set back into his place.

At night, when everyone was asleep, he and Hermit carried on frantically training their arms—the less they believed that it would lead to anything, the greater the effort they applied. Their arms had grown so much that it was no longer possible to exercise with the pieces of iron Hermit had extracted from the food and water troughs when he dismantled them—the members of the community were still fasting and now looked almost transparent—because as soon they began waving their arms, their feet parted from the ground and they had to stop. This was the difficulty that Hermit had once warned Six-Toes about, but they found a way round it: Hermit knew how to strengthen his muscles by means of static exercises, and he taught Six-Toes how. The green gates were already visible beyond the Wall of the World, and Hermit had calculated that there were only ten eclipses left till the Day of Judgement. The gods didn't scare Six-Toes too much now, he'd grown used to their constant attention, accepting it with disdainful humility. His mental balance had been restored and, to amuse himself a little, he began giving dark, almost unintelligible sermons which shook his flock to the core. Once he recalled One-Eye's tale of the underground universe and in a burst of inspiration he described the preparation of the soup for a hundred and sixty demons dressed in green uniforms in such minute detail that by the end of it not only was he himself half-scared to death, but he had seriously alarmed Hermit into the bargain. Many members of the flock learned this sermon by heart, and it became known as "The Revelation of the Blue Ribbon"—this was Six-Toes' sacred title. After this even the former high priests stopped eating and spent hours at a time running round the half-ruined troughs, trying desperately to work off their fat.

Since Hermit and Six-Toes were both eating for two, Hermit had to invent a special dogma of impeccable infallibility, which put a swift end to any whispered murmurs of dissent.

But while Six-Toes rapidly regained his balance after the shock they had experienced, something seemed to be wrong with Hermit. As if Six-Toes' depression had been transferred to him, he became more withdrawn with every passing hour.

Once he said to Six-Toes: "You know, if we don't pull this off, I'm going into Shop Number One along with the rest of them."

Before Six-Toes could open his mouth to object, Hermit stopped him: "And since it's certain we won't pull it off, we can regard the whole thing as settled."

Six-Toes suddenly realized that what he had been about to say was quite pointless. He couldn't change someone else's mind, all he could do was express his own affection for Hermit, so whatever he might say the meaning would be the same. Earlier he probably wouldn't have been able to resist indulging in pointless chatter, but recently something in him had changed. He simply nodded, then moved away, and deliberately immersed himself in contemplation. Soon he came back and said: "I'll go with you."

"No," said Hermit, "you mustn't do that, no matter what. Now you know almost everything that I do, and you have to stay alive and take a disciple. Perhaps at least he will come close to learning how to fly."

"Do you want to leave me alone?" Six-Toes asked irritably. "With these cattle?"

He pointed to the members of the flock, who had stretched themselves out on the ground at the beginning of the prophets' conversation—identical exhausted and trembling bodies covered the ground for almost as far as they could see.

Hermit looked down at his friend's feet with a chuckle. "Tell me, do you remember what you were like before we met?"

Six-Toes thought for a moment and felt embarrassed. "No," he said, "I don't remember. Honestly, I don't remember."

"All right," said Hermit, "you do whatever you think best."

And that was the end of the conversation.

The days remaining until the end flew by. One morning, when the flock had only just opened its eyes, Hermit and Six-Toes noticed that the green gates, which yesterday had seemed far away, were already towering up over the Wall of the World. They glanced at each other and Hermit said: "Today we'll make our last attempt. The last attempt, because tomorrow there won't be anyone left to make another one. We'll go over to the Wall of the World so that this hubbub can't distract us, and we'll try to get from there to the dome of the troughs. If we don't manage it, then we can say our farewells to the world."

"How is that done?" Six-Toes asked by force of habit.

Hermit stared at him in astonishment.

"How should I know how it's done?" he said.

Everyone was told that the prophets were going to communicate with the gods. Soon Hermit and Six-Toes found themselves beside the Wall of the World and they sat down with their backs against it.

"Remember," said Hermit, "you have to imagine that you're already there, and then. . . ."

Six-Toes closed his eyes, focused all his attention on his arms and began thinking about the rubber hose-pipe that hung down to the roof of the troughs. Gradually he fell into a trance, and he had the distinct feeling that the hose-pipe was right beside him and he could reach out his hand to touch it. On previous occasions Six-Toes had always been in a hurry to open his eyes, and he'd always found himself still sitting in the same place, but this time he decided to try something new. "If I slowly bring my arms together," he thought, "so that they wrap round the hose, what then?" Cautiously, trying hard to maintain the certainty he had attained that the hose-pipe was close beside him, he began to move his arms towards each other. And when they closed together on the hose-pipe, where previously there had been only empty space, he began screeching at the top of his voice: "I did it! I did it!"

He opened his eyes.

"Quiet, you fool," said Hermit, who was standing in front of him, and whose leg he was clutching. "Look."

Six-Toes leapt to his feet and looked around. The gates of Shop Number One stood wide open, towering over them as they glided slowly past.

"We've arrived. Let's walk back."

On the way back they didn't say a word. The belt of the conveyor was moving at the same speed as Hermit and Six-Toes were walking, but in the opposite direction, so the entrance to Shop Number One was always there beside them. And when they reached their places of honor beside the two troughs, the entrance moved over and past them.

Hermit called one of the flock to him.

"Listen," he said, "only keep calm! Go and tell the others

that the Day of Judgment has arrived. Do you see how dark the
sky has grown?"

"And what shall we do now?" the other asked hopefully.

"Everyone must sit on the ground and do this," said Hermit,
covering his eyes with his hands. "And don't try to peep, or we
can't guarantee anything. And be sure to keep quiet."

At first even so there was a great hubbub, but it quickly died
away and everyone sat on the ground as Hermit had said.

"Well, then," said Six-Toes, "shall we say our goodbyes to
the world?"

"Yes," answered Hermit. "You go first."

Six-Toes stood up, glanced around him, sighed, and sat back
down again.

"That's it?" Hermit asked.

Six-Toes nodded.

"Now it's my turn," said Hermit, rising to his feet. He threw
back his head and shouted with all his might: "Goodbye, world!"

IX

"Listen to that one cackle," said a voice of thunder. "Which one
was it? That one clucking over there?"

"No," said a different voice, "the one beside him."

Two huge faces appeared above the Wall of the World. The
gods.

"What a bunch of crap," said the first face with disappointment. "I don't see what we can do with this lot. Half-dead already, every one of them."

An immense arm clad in a blood-spattered white sleeve
coated in down reached out at tremendous speed across the world
to touch the twin troughs.

"Semyon, fuck you, are you blind? Their feed system's broken!"

"There wasn't anything wrong with it before," a deep bass

voice replied. "I checked everything at the beginning of the month. What now, are we going to slaughter them?"

"No. Turn the conveyor on and move up another container, and make sure you get that feed system fixed tomorrow. It's a miracle they haven't all croaked. . . ."

"Okay, okay."

"What about this one, with the six toes, do you want both feet?"

"Yeah, cut 'em both off."

"I wanted one for myself."

Hermit turned to Six-Toes, who was listening carefully but not understanding very much.

"Listen," he said, "it seems they want to—"

At that very moment that white arm hurtled across the sky once again and clutched Six-Toes.

Six-Toes didn't hear what Hermit was trying to tell him. The huge hand grabbed him and plucked him from the ground, and then he was facing a large chest with a fountain pen sticking out of its pocket, a shirt-collar and, finally, a pair of huge bulging eyes that stared fixedly at him.

"Hey, look at the wings on him! Like an eagle," said the giant mouth with its yellow, irregular teeth.

Six-Toes had long ago grown used to being handled by the gods, but this time the hands that held him gave off a strange, frightening vibration. All he could make out of the conversation was that they were talking about his arms or about his legs, but then suddenly he heard Hermit shouting up at him like a madman.

"Six-Toes, run for it! Peck him in the face!"

For the first time ever, he heard despair in Hermit's voice, and Six-Toes felt scared, so scared that his every move acquired a somnambulistic precision. He pecked with all his might at the goggling eyes and at the same time he began beating at the god's sweaty face from both sides with incredibly fast movements.

There was a roar so loud that Six-Toes felt it not as a sound, but as pressure against the entire surface of his body. The god's fingers released their grip and a moment later Six-Toes realized that he was up under the ceiling, hanging in the air without any support. At first he couldn't understand what was happening, then he saw that out of sheer repetition he was still flapping his arms to and fro and this was what was holding him up. From up here he could see the true shape of Shop Number One: it was a section of the conveyor, walled in on both sides, runnning beside a long wooden table covered in red and brown blotches, scattered with down and feathers and piles of clear plastic bags. The world in which Hermit still remained was no more than an octagonal container filled with tiny, motionless bodies. Six-Toes could not see Hermit, but he was certain that Hermit could see him.

"Hey," he shouted, flying round in circles just under the ceiling. "Hermit! Come up here, quick! Flap your arms as fast as you can!"

There was a movement down below and Hermit's form gradually grew larger as it came nearer, until he appeared there beside him. He circled a few times after Six-Toes and then shouted: "Let's land over there!"

When Six-Toes flew up to the square patch of dim, milky light, dissected by a narrow cross, Hermit was already sitting on the window sill.

"The wall," he said when Six-Toes landed beside him, "the wall, it shines."

Outwardly Hermit appeared calm but Six-Toes knew him well enough to see that he was shaken by what was happening. Six-Toes felt the same. Suddenly the realization hit him. "Listen," he shouted, "that was flying! We were flying!"

Hermit nodded. "I realized that already," he said. "The truth's so simple it could make you weep."

Meanwhile the disorderly fluttering movement of the figures below had settled down somewhat, and they could see two gods in white coats restraining their companion, who was holding his hand to his face.

"That bastard! He's put my eye out!" the third god was yelling. "The bastard!"

"What's a bastard?" Six-Toes asked.

"It's a way of invoking one of the elemental forces," Hermit answered. "The word doesn't have any real meaning of its own."

"What elemental force is he invoking?" Six-Toes asked.

"We'll soon see," Hermit said.

While Hermit was speaking, the god shrugged off the hands that were holding him back, dashed across to the wall, wrenched down the red fire extinguisher, and hurled it at them where they sat on the window sill. He did it all so quickly that no one could stop him, and Hermit and Six-Toes barely managed to fly off in opposite directions.

There was a ringing sound, followed by a clang. The fire extinguisher broke the window and then disappeared, and a gust of fresh air swept past them, which immediately made clear what a terrible stench there had been before. An intense bright light flooded in.

"Fly for it," Hermit shrieked, instantly losing his former imperturbability. "Move it! Go!"

He flew away from the window, picked up speed, turned back, folded his wings, and disappeared into the beam of hot yellow light pouring in through the hole in the painted glass together with the wind and the new, unfamiliar sounds.

Six-Toes circled, picking up speed. Down below he caught one last glimpse of the octagonal container, the table awash with blood, and the gods waving their arms in the air; then he folded in his wings and whistled through the gap in the window.

For a second he was blinded by the brightness of the light, and then his eyes adjusted. Ahead and above, he caught sight of a circle of yellow-white light too bright to look at even out of the corner of his eye. Higher still in the sky was the black speck that was Hermit. He circled so that Six-Toes could catch up with him, and soon they were flying side by side.

Six-Toes looked around. Far below them was a huge, ugly,

grey building with only a few windows, all painted over. One was broken. The colors of everything around it were so pure and bright that Six-Toes had to look up to stop himself from going out of his mind.

Flying was very easy; it required no more effort than walking. They climbed higher and higher, and soon everything below them was no more than a pattern of colored squares and blotches.

Six-Toes turned his head to look at Hermit.

"Where are we going?" he shouted

"To the South," Hermit replied briefly.

"What's that?" Six-Toes asked.

"I don't know," answered Hermit, "but it's that way."

He gestured with his wing in the direction of the huge glowing circle; only its color resembled what they had once called the lights of heaven.

Crystal World

Here is the third upon the way.
Oh, dear friend, is this you
In the crumpled cap crowning that gaze of tin?
— Alexander Blok

ANYONE WHO HAPPENED to sniff cocaine on October 24th, 1917, on the deserted and inhuman avenues of St. Petersburg, knows for certain that man is not the king of creation. The king of creation would not have curved his palm into the likeness of a Hindu mudra in an attempt to protect the tiny launching pad on his thumbnail from the dank wind. The king of creation would not have used his other hand to prop up the hood that was determined to flop over his eyes. And the king of creation most definitely would not have stooped to gripping in his teeth the stinking leather reins of the stupid Russian horse that was threatening at any second to commit what Merezhkovsky had long before defined as the most boorish of all acts.

"Don't you ever get sick of it, Yury? That's the fifth time you've snorted that stuff today," said Nikolai, in the melancholy realization that his comrade was not going to offer him any this time either.

Yury hid the small mother-of-pearl box away in the pocket of his greatcoat, thought for a second, and suddenly kicked his boots hard against the flanks of his horse.

"H-h-h-ha! And after him the bronze horseman rode," he roared, and set off into the distance with a heavy clattering of hooves along the dark and empty Shpalernaya Street. Then, having somehow persuaded his horse to stop and turn back, he galloped towards Nikolai. On the way he lashed at the signboard of a chemist's shop with an imaginary saber. He even attempted to get his horse to rear up on its hind legs, but its only response was to squat down as firmly as possible and creep all the way across the street to a confectioner's window covered with rows of identical yellow posters for lemonade: a mustachioed hero with the St. George Cross on his chest, stooping slightly to avoid the shrapnel from a shell that has just exploded in the sky, drinks from a tall goblet under the gaze of two very vaguely delineated but beautiful nurses. Nikolai had already discussed the idiotic vulgarity of this poster with someone or other: it hung all over the city, side by side with the Social Revolutionary and Bolshevik broadsheets. Now for some reason it reminded him of Pyotr Ouspensky's leaflet on the fourth dimension, printed on rotten newsprint, and he imagined a horse's ass backing out of nowhere to knock the lemonade out of the weary warrior's hand.

Yury finally gained control of his horse, and after a few pirouettes in the center of the street he rode up to Nikolai.

"And note," he said, continuing their interrupted conversation, "any culture is precisely a paradoxical unity of things which at first glance have no logical connection. Of course, there are parallels: the wall that encircles an ancient city and a round coin, for instance, or the rapid mastery of huge distances with the help of trains, howitzers, the telegraph. And so forth. But the most important thing, of course, is something quite different, it is the manifestation every time of a certain indissoluble unity, a certain principle which cannot be formulated in itself, despite its extreme simplicity. . . ."

"We've already talked about that," Nikolai said coolly, "the indefinable principle which is identically reflected in every phenomenon of a culture."

"That's right. And this cultural principle has a certain set period of existence, approximately one thousand years. And within this period it passes through all the same stages as a human being: a culture can be young, old, or dying. Dying is the stage we're in now. That's particularly obvious here in Russia. All of this"—Yury gestured towards the red calico banner with its inscription HURRAH FOR THE CONSTITUENT ASSEMBLY stretched between two lampposts—"is already the death throes. Even the beginning of decomposition."

They rode on for a while without speaking. Nikolai occasionally glanced to each side: it was as though life on the street had become extinct, and if not for the few windows that were lit, he could have believed that everyone who embodied the old culture had died along with it. It was more than an hour since they had come on duty, and they hadn't seen a single person on the street, which had made it quite impossible to carry out Captain Prikhodov's orders.

"There's a rumor that Lenin will try to get to the Smolny to lead the rebellion. So don't let a single civilian whore down Shpalernaya in the direction of Smolny," the captain had said when the sentries were posted, glancing significantly at Yury. "Clear?"

"How would you like us to take that order, captain," Yury asked him, "in its literal sense?"

"In every possible sense, Cadet Popovich, in every possible sense."

"But what does this Lenin look like?"

"Don't know."

In order for them not to let anybody down Shpalernaya in the direction of Smolny, however, there had to be a third person in addition to the two cadets, someone trying to make his way in that direction. But there was no one, and so far their sentry duty

had been filled with Yury's rather confused account of a manu-
script by some German, which Nikolai was unable to read for
himself because of his poor knowledge of the language.

"What's his name again? Spuller?"

"Spengler," repeated Yury.

"What's the book called?"

"Nobody knows. I told you, it hasn't been published yet. It
was a typed copy of the first few chapters. They brought it in
through Switzerland."

"I must remember it," muttered Nikolai, and immediately
forgot the German surname once again; the meaningless word
"Spuller," however, became firmly fixed in his mind. This sort
of thing happened to him all the time. Whenever he wanted to
commit something to memory, what he wanted to remember
evaporated completely and what was left in his head were the
various aids he had constructed to help him retain it, and these
lodged there very firmly indeed. His attempts to recall the
name of the bearded German anarchist whose works so engrossed his schoolgirl sister immediately summoned up Marcus
Aurelius's monument. And when he wanted to remember the
address of some house, he uncovered the date 1825 and five
profiles, either from the label of a cognac bottle or from a theo-
sophical journal—he wasn't quite sure. He gave one more try at
recalling the German name: this time "Spuller" was followed
by the word "Singer," and then "parabellum." The third word
was totally out of place, and the second couldn't be the name
he needed, because it didn't start with the sound "sh." Then
Nikolai decided to try cunning. He would remember the word
"Spuller" as one resembling the word that he had lost; the idea
was that "Spuller" would be forgotten, and the name should
take its place.

Just when Nikolai had decided to ask his comrade again, he
suddenly noticed a dark figure creeping along the wall from the
direction of Liteiny Prospect, and he tugged at Yury's sleeve.
Yury started and looked around. He saw the figure and tried to

whistle. The sound that emerged was not a whistle exactly, but it certainly did sound like a warning.

The stranger, a gentleman, realizing that he had been noticed, separated himself from the wall, and moving into the bright patch of light under a street lamp, made himself entirely visible. At first glance he appeared to be about fifty or a little older, and he was dressed in a dark coat with a velvet collar, with a bowler on his head. The face, with its semi-Chekhovian beard and broad cheekbones, would have been quite unremarkable, if not for the cunning expression of the eyes, which were screwed up as though they had just winked at two different people in different directions for quite different reasons. In his right hand the gentleman held a cane, which he waved to and fro to indicate that he was simply walking about and minding his own business, doing nobody any harm and not intending to: in general, he knew nothing about all these outrageous goings-on. To Nikolai's metaphorically inclined way of thinking, he looked like a horse thief whose specialty was thoroughbreds worth thousands.

"Cheers, wads," he said in a familiar, even somewhat insolent tone, "how's wife in the awmy?"

"Just where would you happen to be going, sir?" Nikolai inquired coldly.

"Me? I'm just taking a walk. Wound about. You see, I've been dwinking coffee all day, and I got this tewible aching in my heart this evening, so I thought I'd better get a bweath of air. . . ."

"So you're just taking a walk?" Nikolai asked.

"Yes I am. . . . Why, is that forbidden?"

"No, of course not. But we have to ask you: could you please walk in the other direction? It's all the same to you where you take the air, surely?"

"It is, it is," agreed the gentleman, and then suddenly frowned. "But then this weally is an outwage. I'm used to stwolling to and fwo wight here on Shpawernaya. . . ." He gestured with his cane, to and fro.

Yury swayed slightly in his saddle, and the gentleman turned his attention to him, so that Yury felt the need to say something.

"Our orders," he said, "are not to let a single civilian whore down towards Smolny."

The gentleman took lively offense at this and thrust his little beard up and out.

"How dare you? You. . . . Why, I'll expose you in the newspapers, in *New Time* . . . ," he began jabbering. It was immediately obvious that if he did have any connections with the press, they were certainly not with *New Time*. "Such insolence. Do you have any idea who you're talking to?"

His outraged tone contradicted the readiness with which he was already backing out of the patch of light into the darkness. The words suggested that a long and serious argument was beginning, while his movements demonstrated that he was poised not merely to retreat, but to take to his heels and make a run for it.

"There's a state of emergency in the city," Nikolai shouted after him, "take your fresh air from your window for a couple of days!"

The gentleman, retreating silently and swiftly, soon disappeared into the darkness.

"Despicable sort," said Nikolai, "definitely a crook. Those shifty eyes. . . ."

Yury nodded absent-mindedly. The two cadets rode as far as the corner of Liteiny Prospect and turned back, a maneuver which cost Yury some effort. In managing his horse he demonstrated all the skills of the experienced cyclist, holding the reins as wide apart as handlebars, and when he needed to stop, he jerked his feet in the stirrups, as though pedalling backwards on a Dunlop semi-racer.

A fine, dismal drizzle began to fall, and Nikolai pulled up the hood of his cloak as well, so that it became quite impossible to tell the two of them apart.

"What d'you think, Yury," Nikolai asked after a while, "will Kerensky be able to hold on for long?"

"I don't think about it at all," answered Yury. "What difference does it make? If it's not one of them it's another. You tell me how you feel in all of this."

"How d'you mean?" Just for a moment Nikolai thought Yury meant his military uniform.

"Well, look here," said Yury, indicating something ahead of them with the gesture of a man sowing grain, "somewhere out there there's a war going on and people are dying. They've overthrown the emperor, turned every damn thing topsy-turvy. There are Bolsheviks chuckling on every corner, chewing sunflower seeds, cooks in red armbands, drunken sailors. Everything's in motion now, as though some dam has burst. And there you are, Nikolai Muromtsev, standing there in the top boots of your spirit, right in the very middle of this great sloppy mess. How do you understand what you are?"

Nikolai thought it over. "I've never really tried to express it. I just carry on living, that's all."

"But do you have a mission?"

"What d'you mean, a mission?" Nikolai answered, a little embarrassed by the question. "Good God, what will you come out with next?"

Yury tugged on his gun-strap to straighten it, and the butt of the carbine rose up behind his back and looked like the head of a small steel turkey carefully listening to their conversation.

"Everyone has a mission," said Yury, "you just have to not treat the word too solemnly. For instance, Charles the Twelfth fought wars all his life, against us and everybody else, he minted all kinds of medals in his own honor, built ships, seduced women. He went hunting and he got drunk. And meanwhile in some Russian village, let's say there was a young shepherd growing up, and his wildest dream was to get a new pair of birchbark sandals. He of course never thought that he might have any kind of mission, he didn't even know this word existed. Then he ended up in the army, he was given a gun and more or less learned how to shoot. Perhaps he didn't really even learn how to shoot, but only how to stick the muzzle out of a trench and pull the trigger. And then one day he stuck the muzzle out of his trench and pulled the trigger, just when the magnificent Charles the Twelfth on his royal charger was riding across the bullet's line of fire. And he hit him right on the crown. . . ."

Yury swung his arm to demonstrate the fall of the dead Swedish king from his galloping horse.

"The most interesting thing," he continued, "is that a person usually never realizes what his mission is, and he won't realize it until the moment he commits that act for which he was put on this earth. Let's say he believes he's a composer and his task is to write music, but in fact the only purpose of his existence is to fall under a cart on the way to the conservatory."

"What for?"

"Well, for instance, so that a lady riding in a cab will be frightened into having a miscarriage and humanity will be spared a new Genghis Khan. Or so that someone looking out the window will have a new idea. It could be anything."

"Well, if you put it like that," said Nikolai, "then of course everyone has a mission. Only it's impossible to ever find out what it is."

"No, there are ways," Yury said, and then said no more.

"What ways?"

"Well, there's a certain Doctor Steiner in Switzerland. . . . Oh, never mind," Yury waved his hand dismissively, and Nikolai realized it would be better not to pester him with questions for the moment.

Shpalernaya Street was dark and mysterious, as dark and mysterious as Yury's words about the German doctor. Everything was shrouded in mist, Nikolai felt sleepy, and his head began to droop. In the tiny intervals between hoofbeats he fell asleep and then woke up again, and every time he had a brief dream. At first the dreams were chaotic and meaningless: unfamiliar faces came drifting out of the darkness, squinted at him in amazement and disappeared; there were glimpses of dark pagodas on snow-clad mountain peaks, and Nikolai remembered that this was a monastery, and he seemed to know something about it, but then the vision disappeared. Then he dreamed that he and Yury were riding along the high bank of a river and gazing at a black cloud creeping in from the west and already covering half the sky, but it wasn't really him and Yury, it was two other soldiers, and Nikolai felt he was just about to grasp something really important, but he woke up, and he was back in the middle of Shpalernaya.

There were only five or six windows lit in the houses, which loomed like the walls of that deep dark fissure beyond which, if the ancient poet is to be believed, lies the entrance to Hell. "What a dreary city," Nikolai thought as he listened to the wind whistling down the drainpipes, "how can people go on having children here, and giving each other flowers, and laughing. . . . But then I live here, too. . . ." Somehow the thought astonished him. The drizzle had stopped, but that didn't make Nikolai feel any more comfortable on this street. He dozed off again in the saddle, and this time he had no dreams.

He was woken by music from the darkness. At first the melody was unclear but then, as the cadets approached the source (a lighted window on the ground floor of a brown three-storey building with a cupid blowing on a horn over the door), they could make out the waltz "On the Hills of Manchuria," arranged in the usual fashion for wind instruments.

"The silence of the night, with the rustling of the kaoliang. . . ."

They heard a powerful male voice singing over the soft, flat music from the gramophone. The sharply defined shadow of the voice's owner lay on the painted glass of the window. Judging from the peaked cap, he was an officer. He was balancing a plate on one hand and waving a fork in time to the music. On some beats the fork blurred and swelled into the immense shadow of some fantastic insect.

"Sleep, my friends, your country remembers you. . . ."

Nikolai thought about his friends.

When they had gone a dozen or so yards further the music

stopped, and Nikolai again began thinking about the strange things Yury had been saying.

"What ways are there?" he asked.

"What are you talking about?"

"What you were just saying. Ways to find out about your mission."

"Oh, it's all nonsense," said Yury, and he waved his hand dismissively again. He stopped his horse, carefully gripped the reins between his teeth and took the small mother-of-pearl box out of his pocket. Nikolai rode on a bit, then stopped and looked inquiringly at his comrade.

Yury covered his face with his hands, twitched his nose and stared bemusedly at Nikolai. Nikolai laughed and raised his eyes to heaven, thinking, "Surely the swine will offer me some this time?"

"Would you like some cocaine?" Yury finally asked.

"I'm not really sure," Nikolai answered lazily. "Is it good stuff?"

"Yes."

"Did you get it from Captain Prikhodov?"

"Na-a," said Yury, charging his other nostril, "this came from the Social Revolutionaries. This is what the terrorists sniff before they throw a bomb or shoot someone."

"Aha! That sounds interesting."

Nikolai took out a tiny monogrammed silver spoon from his greatcoat and held it out to Yury, who grasped it by the bowl and thrust the spiral rod of the handle into the mother-of-pearl cocaine box.

"Cheapskate," thought Nikolai, leaning over a long way from his horse as though to deliver a saber blow, and offering his left nostril to his comrade's slightly trembling fingers; Yury held the spoon between his finger and thumb, gripping hard as if he had a tiny, deadly venomous snake by the neck.

The cocaine scorched Nikolai's throat in the usual way. It didn't feel any different from the ordinary sorts, but out of gratitude he tried to run the entire gamut of exaggerated responses across his face. He didn't straighten up immediately, hoping that his right nostril would be remembered as well, but Yury suddenly snapped the box shut, shoved it into his pocket, and nodded towards Liteiny Prospect.

Nikolai straightened up in the saddle. Someone was walking towards them from the Prospect but at that distance he couldn't tell who. Nikolai swore quietly in English and galloped towards the figure. An old woman wearing a hat with a dark veil was walking slowly and cautiously along the pavement, as though afraid at every step of tripping over something. Nikolai almost ran her down, but by some miracle he managed to swerve his horse aside at the last moment. The startled woman, pressing herself against the wall of a building, squealed so submissively that Nikolai remembered his grandmother, and felt a brief pang of guilt.

"Madame," he roared, pulling out his saber and saluting, "What are you doing here? Are you aware that there is fighting in the city?"

"Me?" the woman croaked in a hoarse voice. "I should think so!"

"Have you gone crazy then? You could be killed, or robbed. You'll get run over by some Plekhanov in his armored car, he won't think twice about it."

"We'll see who wuns over who," the woman muttered with unexpected vehemence, clenching a pair of rather large fists.

"Madame," Nikolai said, relaxing and putting away his saber, "your high spirits are most praiseworthy, but you should return home immediately, back to your husband and children. Sit by the fireplace and read something amusing, have a glass of wine if you like. But don't come out on the street, I beg you."

"I have to go that way," said the woman, gesturing decisively with her handbag in the direction of the dark fissure leading to hell, which was now definitely at the far end of Shpalernaya.

"What do you want to go there for?"

"My fwend's waiting for me. My companion."

"Then you'll see each other as soon as it's all over," said Yury, riding up to them. "You've been told clearly enough, you can't go on that way. You can go back, but you can't go on."

The woman moved her head from side to side. The dark veil completely concealed her features, and it was impossible to tell which way she was looking.

"Move on, now," Nikolai said gently, "it's almost ten, and then it will be really dangerous out on the street."

"Donnerwetter!" muttered the woman.

Somewhere close by a dog began to howl, and its howling was so filled with anguish and hatred that Nikolai squirmed in his saddle, suddenly aware of how repulsively damp everything was. The woman loitered in an odd fashion under the streetlamp. Nikolai turned his horse and looked inquiringly at Yury.

"Well?" Yury asked

"I'm not sure. I didn't really get enough to judge properly. It seems like the ordinary stuff."

"No, no," said Yury, "I meant the woman. There's something odd about her, I didn't like the look of her at all."

"Neither did I," said Nikolai, turning round to see whether the old woman could hear them, but there was no sign of her.

"And note that they both lisp. That first one, the man, and this woman."

"Well, what of it? Lots of people pronounce their 'r' the French way. All the French do, and the Germans, too, I think. Not quite the same way, though."

"Steiner says that when an event is repeated several times it's a sign from the higher powers."

"Who's Steiner? The doctor who wrote the book about cultures?"

"No, the book was written by Spengler. He's a historian, not a doctor. I saw Doctor Steiner in Switzerland. I used to go to his lectures. A remarkable man. He was the one who told me about the mission. . . ."

Yury sighed.

The cadets rode slowly up Shpalernaya towards Smolny. For a long time the street had felt dead, but only in the sense that with each passing minute it became more difficult to imagine anyone alive behind the black windows, or out on the slippery pavement. In a different sense, a non-human one, the street was becoming more and more alive: the stillness of the caryatids, who went completely unnoticed by day, was now only a pretence, and they watched attentively with their painted eyes as the two friends rode past. The eagles on the pediments were ready at any second to soar up into the air and come swooping down at any second on the two horsemen, and in the plaster cartouches the bearded faces of the warriors smirked and turned to look the other way. The howling in the drainpipes began again, even though they could feel no wind on the street. Up above, where in the daytime there was a broad strip of sky, they could see neither clouds nor stars: a cold, damp gloom sagged down between the two rows of roofs, and wisps of fog crept down the walls. For some reason two or three of the small number of glowing street-lamps had gone out, and the window on the first floor, where the officer was recently singing the tragic and beautiful waltz, was no longer lit either.

"Come on, Yury, give me some cocaine," Nikolai asked at last. Yury, evidently experiencing the same perturbation of spirit, nodded as though Nikolai had said something remarkably profound, and reached into his pocket.

This time Yury was less stingy. When Nikolai lifted his head, he was amazed to observe that his black mood had lifted, and he was on an ordinary nighttime street, perhaps a little dark and gloomy, veiled in a heavy mist, but nonetheless one of the streets on which he had spent his childhood and youth, with the familiar meager decorations on the walls of the houses and the flickering dim streetlamps.

Far away on Liteiny Prospect there was a rifle shot, and then another, and immediately he heard hoofbeats approaching and

the wild shouts of mounted cavalry. Nikolai pulled out his carbine from behind his shoulder: the idea of death at his post
seemed beautiful to him, death with his rifle in his hands and the
taste of blood in his mouth. But Yury remained calm.

"They're ours," he said.

He was right, the horsemen who appeared out of the fog
were dressed in the same uniform as Yury and Nikolai. A second
later they could make out their faces.

At the front, on a young white mare, rode Captain Prikhodov,
the ends of his black moustaches swept upwards, his eyes gleaming bravely, and the frozen lightning bolt of a Caucasian saber
clutched in his hand. Twelve cadets were galloping in close for-
mation behind him.

"Well? Everything all right?"

"Everything's fine, captain!" Yury and Nikolai answered in
unison, drawing themselves up in their saddles.

"There are bandits on Liteiny," said the captain thoughtfully,
"look. . . ." A dull metallic disk attached to a long chain
slapped into Nikolai's palm. It was a watch. He opened it with his
fingernail and looked at the deeply engraved Gothic lettering. He
couldn't make it out, so he handed the watch to Yury.

"From the General . . . From the General Staff," Yury
translated from the German, reading the small letters with difficulty in the semidarkness. "Obviously an award, a trophy. But the
strange thing, captain, is the chain. It's steel. You could lock a
door with it."

He handed the watch back to Nikolai. Although the chain
was thin it was quite remarkably strong. Its links had no joints, as
the entire chain were carved out of a single piece of steel.

"You could strangle someone with it," said the captain. "There
are three corpses on Liteiny. Two of them right on the corner, an invalid and a nurse, strangled and then undressed. Either they were
dumped there, or that's actually where . . . most likely they were
dumped there, the nurse couldn't have been carrying a man with no
legs. . . . But so brutal! Even at the front I never saw anything

like it. They obviously took the invalid's watch and then used his own chain. . . . There's a huge puddle. . . ."

Meanwhile one of the cadets had separated from the group and ridden over to Yury. It was Vaska Zivers, a great lover of horseracing and artillery. In college he was disliked for excessive pedantry and his poor Russian, but he was on good terms with Yury, who spoke German well.

". . . A hundred yards further on," the captain was saying, slapping his saber against his boot, "a third body in a gateway. . . . A woman, also almost naked . . . and marks from the chain. . . ."

Vaska touched Yury's shoulder, and without taking his eyes off the captain, Yury nodded and held out a curved palm, into which Vaska quickly placed a tiny bundle. All of this took place behind Yury's back, but even so it did not escape the captain's attention.

"What's all this, Cadet Zivers?" he said, interrupting his own monologue. "What are you doing over there?"

"Captain! In four minutes we have to change the guard at Nikolaevsky Station!" Vaska replied, saluting.

"At a trot, forward!" roared the captain. "About-turn! On to Liteiny! We won't get by Smolny quickly."

The cadets turned around and dashed away into the fog. Captain Prikhodov reined in his prancing mare and shouted back to Yury and Nikolai:

"Don't separate! Let no one through without a pass. Don't go out onto Liteiny or stick your noses out at Smolny! Clear? Change at ten-thirty!"

He disappeared after the cadets. For a few more seconds they could hear the hoofbeats, then all was silence, and it was impossible to believe that there had been so many people on the damp, dark street.

"From the General Staff," Nikolai muttered, tossing the round silvery object up and down on his palm. In his haste the captain had forgotten the strange thing he had found.

The watch was shaped like a small shell. On its face were three hands, and on the side three small knobs for winding. Nikolai carefully pressed the top one and almost dropped the watch on the road when it began to play music—the first few notes of some majestic German melody. Nikolai recognized it immediately, but he didn't know what it was called.

"*The Appassionata*," said Yury. "Ludwig van Beethoven. My brother told me that the Germans play it on their mouth organs before an attack. Instead of a march."

He opened Vaska's little bundle, which proved to consist mostly of paper. Inside there were five ampules with unevenly welded necks. Yury shrugged.

"That Prikhodov's getting tricky," he said, "now he's seeing through people. But what can we do with these without a syringe. . . . Some pal Vaska is. Takes cocaine and gives you ephedrine. Have you got a syringe on you?"

"Of course I have," Nikolai answered in a dismal voice. He didn't want any ephedrine. He wanted to go back to the barracks, hand in his greatcoat to the drying room, lie down on his bed, and fix his gaze on the familiar spot on the ceiling. When he was drowsy it turned into a map of the city, or a rapacious, bearded mongol face, or an inverted headless eagle. Nikolai could never remember anything more than the vague echoes of his dreams. With Captain Prikhodov's departure the street was once again transformed into the fissure leading to hell. Strange things happened. On the gateway to one of the houses someone had managed to put a padlock; several empty bottles with bright yellow labels now stood in the very middle of the road; and an immense poster had appeared, hanging crookedly above the ads for lemonade in the confectioner's window, with the first line consisting of the word "Comrades" in big letters and several exclamation marks. Almost all of the streetlamps had gone out—there were only two still burning, opposite each other. Nikolai thought that some soused decadent from The Wandering Dog who could no longer take things simply for what they are, might take the lamps for a mystically illuminated gateway guarded by some monstrous beast that could crawl out of the gloom and consume the entire world at any moment.

"Comrades," he said to himself, repeating the first line of the poster.

Somewhere the dogs began barking again, and Nikolai began to feel miserable. A cold wind blew up, rattled the tin roofs, and then hurtled away again, leaving behind a strange and unpleasant sound, a piercing, distant scraping from somewhere in the direction of Liteiny. The sound kept disappearing and then reappearing, gradually drawing nearer all the time, as though Shpalernaya Street was covered with a thick layer of broken glass, and a huge nail was slowly being scraped across it, stopping every now and then as it approached those last two points of light.

"What is it?" Nikolai asked in a stupid voice.

"I don't know," Yury answered, peering into the black, swirling fog.

"We'll soon see."

The scraping halted for a short time and then they heard it again, very close now, and one of the wreaths of mist that was especially dense and dark separated from the gloom that had settled in between the houses. As it came closer, it gradually assumed the form of a strange being: the upper part, down to the shoulders, was a human being, but the lower part was something weird and massive that writhed as it moved. It was the lower part that gave out the repulsive scraping sound. The strange creature was mumbling quietly to itself in two different voices, a male voice that groaned and a female voice that comforted. The woman's voice came from the upper part, and the man's voice came from the lower. The being with two voices cleared its throat, moved into the zone of light, stopped, and only then, as it seemed to Nikolai, assumed its final form.

Sitting in front of the cadets was a man in a wheelchair. He was wrapped in copious bandages and bedecked with medals. Even his face was bandaged. Between the strips of gauze only his bald bulging forehead and one gleaming, reddish, screwed-up eye could be seen. The man was holding an old-looking guitar decorated with silk ribbons of various colors.

Standing behind the wheelchair and clutching its back with swollen fingers was a grey-haired middle-aged woman in a tattered jacket trimmed with fur. She was not exactly fat, but somehow swollen, like a sack full of grain. Her eyes were round and wild; and they were obviously not seeing Shpalernaya Street, but something else which could not even be guessed at. A small cap with a red ribbon was perched crookedly on her head. Probably it was pinned there, because according to the laws of physics it should have fallen off.

Several seconds went by in silence, then Yury licked his dry lips and said: "Your pass."

The invalid shifted in his chair, looked up at the nurse, and mumbled something anxiously. The nurse came out from behind the wheelchair, leaned towards the cadets, and put her hands on her knees. Nikolai was amazed to see patched soldier's boots beneath her blue skirt.

"Have you no shame?" she asked in a quiet voice, fixing Yury with a piercing gaze. "He has a head wound, he got it fighting for you. Where would he get a pass?"

"A head wound, you say?" Yury said thoughtfully. "But now he seems to have recovered. Your pass."

The woman looked around in confusion.

The invalid in the wheelchair jangled the strings of the guitar, and a slow vibrating sound filled the street. It seemed to urge the nurse on, and she bent forward again and said:

"Don't you be angry now, son. . . . Don't you be angry just because I said something wrong, but we have to go through. If only you knew this man sitting here. A hero. Lieutenant Krivotykin of the Preobrazhensky regiment. A hero of the Brusilov breach. His comrade in battle is off to the front tomorrow, and he might not come back. Let us through, they must see each other. You understand, don't you?"

"The Preobrazhensky regiment, you say?"

The invalid nodded, clutched the guitar to his chest, and began to play. He played in a strange manner, as if the instrument were red-hot, striking the strings cautiously and pulling his fingers back quickly, but Nikolai recognized the melody. It was the Preobrazhensky regimental march. Another strange thing was that the sound hole, which is always round in a guitar, was shaped like a pentagram. That must have been the reason for the low, heartrending tone.

When the invalid had finished playing, Yury said in a flat, expressionless voice: "But the Preobrazhensky regiment wasn't involved in the the Brusilov breach."

The invalid mumbled something, gesturing towards the nurse with his guitar. She turned to face him, evidently trying to make out what he wanted, but she didn't understand until the invalid drew that low vibrating sound from his instrument once again, and then she suddenly got the idea.

"Why don't you believe him, son? The lieutenant asked to be posted to the front, he served in the Third Amur Division, in the mounted battalion. . . ."

The invalid in the wheelchair nodded in a dignified manner.

"He took an Austrian battery with twenty horsemen. He has the orders from the Supreme Commander-in-Chief," the nurse said reproachfully, and turned back to the invalid. "Show him, lieutenant. . . ."

The invalid put his hand into the side pocket of his frock coat and pulled out something that he gave to the nurse. She gave the sheet of paper to Yury, who passed it on to Nikolai without reading it. Nikolai unfolded it and read aloud:

"*Lieutenant Krivotykin, fourth battalion, Third Amur Division. I order you to attack the enemy front from the village of Onut to the crossroads to the north, striking the main blow between the villages of Onut and Cherny Potok in order to take Height 236 at dairy farm and the northern slope of Height 265. Signed, Corps Commander Artillery General Barantsev.*"

"What else can you show me?" Yury asked.

The invalid put his hand into his pocket and took out a watch, and for a moment Nikolai felt confused. The nurse handed the watch to Yury, who looked at it and passed it to Nikolai. "I could open a jewelry store if this keeps up," thought Nikolai as he opened its golden cover. "Two watches in an hour." The inside of the lid was engraved:

"To Lieutenant Krivotykin for a courageous raid. General Barantsev."

The invalid quietly strummed the Preobrazhensky march on his guitar and squinted at something in the far distance, clearly thinking of his comrades in battle.

"A good watch. But we can show you a better one," said Yury. He took the silver seashell out of his pocket, swung it to and fro on its chain, and pressed its small ribbed knob.

The watch began to play its tune.

Nikolai had never seen music, not even music of genius, have such a powerful and immediate effect on anyone. The invalid covered his face with his hands for a second, as though he couldn't believe such music could have been written by man, and then he did something very strange. He leapt out of his wheelchair and ran off in the direction of Liteiny Prospect. The nurse followed him, clattering over the road in her soldier's boots. Nikolai took his carbine from his shoulder, fiddled with the safety catch, and fired into the air.

"Halt!" he shouted.

The nurse turned as she ran and fired several shots at them from a pistol. The bullets, whining as they ricocheted, scattered across the road the broken glass of a hairdresser's window, where only a moment earlier an art nouveau-style girl painted in gold had been gazing out at the world through startled eyes. Nikolai lowered the barrel of his rifle and shot twice at random into the mist. The fugitives were out of sight.

"Why do they all want to get to Smolny so badly?" Yury

asked, trying to sound calm. He hadn't got off a single shot, and was still holding the watch in his hand.

"I don't know," said Nikolai. "Probably they want to get to the Bolsheviks, where they can get alcohol and cocaine cheap."

"Have you ever bought any?"

"No," answered Nikolai, slinging his carbine back behind his shoulder. "I've just heard about it. Never mind that. You were going to tell me about your mission, about Doctor Spuller. . . ."

"Steiner," Yury corrected him. Powerful sensations had made him feel talkative. "He's a visionary. When I was in Dornach, I used to go to his lectures. I sat as close as I could, and even took notes. After every lecture he was surrounded immediately and led away, so there was no chance to talk to him. Anyway, I didn't particularly want to. Then he started looking at me during his lectures. He talked and talked and then he'd stop and stare at me. I didn't know what to think. Then one day he came up to me and said: 'You and I have to talk, young man.' We went to a restaurant and sat down at a table. He began telling me very strange things, about the Apocalypse, about the invisible world, and so on. And then he said that I was marked with a special sign and I would play an immensely important role in history. That whatever I might do, in the spiritual sense I was on some kind of guard duty, defending the world against an ancient demon that I had already fought before."

"When could you have done that?" asked Nikolai.

"In previous incarnations. He—not the demon, Doctor Steiner—said that only I could stop him, but no one could say whether I would manage it. Not even Doctor Steiner himself. He even showed me an engraving in an old book which he said I was in. There were two men with long hair, each holding a sword in one hand and an hourglass in the other, all dressed in armor, and one of them was supposed to be me."

"Do you believe all that?"

"God only knows," laughed Yury. "All I've done so far is shoot at nurses. And not even me, but you. Well, time for a fix?"

"Why not," agreed Nikolai, and he reached under his great-coat into the chest pocket of his uniform tunic, where he kept the small syringe in its nickel-plated box.

The street was absolutely quiet now. The wind had stopped howling in the drainpipes. The hungry dogs seemed to have quit their gateway and departed. Peace had descended on Shpaler-naya. Even the breaking of the narrow glass necks of the vials could be heard distinctly.

"Two grams," a voice whispered.

"Of course," another voice whispered in reply.

"Open your coat," whispered the first voice. "You'll bend the needle."

"Nonsense," responded the second voice.

"You're crazy," whispered the first voice, "think of your horse. . . ."

"That's all right, she's used to it."

Nikolai raised his head and looked around. It was hard to believe that a St. Petersburg street in autumn could be so beautiful. In the window of a florist's shop there were three tiny pines growing in oak tubs. The street ran steeply uphill, widening as it went. The windows of the upper storeys of the houses reflected a ray of light from the moon that had just appeared in a gap between the buildings. All of this was Russia, and it was so beautiful that tears welled up in Nikolai's eyes.

"We will defend you, crystal world," he whispered, laying his palm on the handle of his saber. Yury was clutching the strap of his carbine tightly by his left shoulder and gazing at the moon as it rushed along the tattered edge of a dark cloud. When it was hidden from sight, he turned a face filled with inspiration to his companion.

"Ephedrine's a wonderful thing," he said.

Nikolai didn't answer. What was there to say? The air moved in and out of his chest differently now, everything around him was different, and even the repulsive drizzle caressed his cheeks.

Thousands of irresolvable questions great and small, which so recently had tormented him, no longer seemed even to exist. His life's center of gravity was altogether elsewhere—but when this elsewhere was revealed, it turned out to be extremely close. It was there in every minute of every day, but it was invisible, the way a picture that hangs on the wall for a long time becomes invisible.

"I grip my crutch with piteous hand," Yury began reciting. "My friend, enamored of the moon, lives in its deception. Here is the third upon the way. . . ."

Nikolai no longer heard his comrade. He was thinking of how he would change his life the very next day. His thoughts were incoherent and sometimes frankly stupid, but very pleasant. He had to begin by getting up at half past five in the morning and dousing himself with cold water, and then there was such a mass of various options to choose from that it was very difficult to settle on anything in particular, and Nikolai began forcing himself to choose, mumbling aloud to himself without being aware of it, and clenching his fists in excitement.

"The fences are like coffins! Filth rots all around, And everything is buried in this accursed desolation!" Yury recited, wiping away the sweat that was beginning to bead his forehead with the sleeve of his greatcoat.

They rode in silence for a while, then Yury began singing some song or other, and Nikolai fell into a strange state of drowsiness. It was strange because it was so very different from sleep, like the state induced by several cups of strong coffee, but accompanied by dreamlike visions. The roadways of Nikolai's childhood appeared before his eyes, overlaid on Shpalernaya Street; the grammar school and the apple tree outside his window; a rainbow over the town; the black ice of a slide and skaters dashing by, illuminated by bright electric light; leafless, century-old lime trees in two rows converging on a house with a colonnade. Then pictures began to appear which seemed familiar, but which he'd actually never seen before. He dreamed of an immense white city crowned with thousands of golden church cupolas that seemed to hang inside a crystal ball, and this city, Nikolai knew for certain, was all of Russia, and he and Yury, who was not quite Yury in the dream, were outside it, dashing through the swirling fog on their steeds to meet the monster—and the most terrible thing about it was the absolute indefiniteness of its form and size, it was a formless swirling mass of emptiness radiating an icy cold.

Nikolai shuddered and opened his eyes wide. A tiny crack had appeared in the armor-plating of his bliss, and a few drops of uncertainty and anguish had seeped in. The crack was growing, and soon the thought of what would happen tomorrow morning (at exactly five-thirty) to change his entire life ceased to bring him any pleasure. After another couple of minutes, when he could see the two lamps flickering on each side of the street, the thought became a distinct and major source of profound suffering.

"Cold turkey," Nikolai was eventually forced to admit to himself. It was strange how the frankness of this conclusion seemed to patch the breach in his soul, and the quantity of suffering in it stopped increasing. But now he had to follow his own thoughts with great care, because any one of them could mark the boundary of an infinite field of endless suffering, which he would like to believe was still far away, but which ephedrine demanded every time for its services. The same thing was clearly happening to Yury, because he turned to Nikolai and spoke in a quick, quiet voice, as though he was trying to conserve the air escaping from his lungs.

"We should have taken it in the gut."

"There wouldn't have been enough," Nikolai answered equally curtly, feeling that he hated his comrade for making him open his mouth.

The horses' hooves made a thick, sickening crunching sound as they walked along. It was the shards of glass from the shop window broken by the ricochet of the revolver bullets.

"Cr-r-rystal world," thought Nikolai, with a feeling of disgust for himself and everything else in the world. His recent visions suddenly seemed so absurd and shameful that he felt like answering the crunching of the glass by grinding his teeth to make the same noise.

Now it was quite clear what was waiting for them up ahead. Cold turkey. At first it lurked somewhere close to the streetlamps, and then, when the streetlamps were close at hand, it withdrew into the swirling fog at the intersection with Liteiny Prospect and bided its time. There was no longer any doubt that cold, wet, and dirty Shpalernaya Street was all that existed in the world, and the only thing they could expect from it was endless gloom and torment.

A small black dog of indeterminate breed ran along the street with its tail held high, barked at the two grey monkeys hunched in the saddles, and darted into a gateway, and then the cold turkey assumed a visible form over near Liteiny and began moving towards them. The form was that of a middle-aged man with a moustache wearing a leather cap and gleaming boots. A typical class-conscious proletarian. The proletarian was pushing along a large yellow cart with the inscription LEMONADE on its sides, and on the front it had the same advertising poster that had infuriated Nikolai even when he was in high spirits; now it seemed like everything vile in the world had been gathered together on a single sheet of paper.

"Your pass," said Yury, squeezing the words out with a painful effort.

"Here you are," said the man solemnly, and he handed Yury a sheet of paper folded in two.

"Let me see. Eino Raikhya . . . Permitted . . . Commandant . . . What have you got in the cart?"

"Lemonade for the watch. Would you like some?"

Two bottles with poisonous yellow labels gleamed in the proletarian's hands. Yury feebly waved them away and dropped the pass, but the proletarian caught it deftly just before it fell into a puddle.

"Lemonade?" Nikolai asked in a stupefied voice. "Where to? What for?"

"You see," replied the proletariat, "I work for Karl Lieb-knecht and Sons, and we have a contract to supply lemonade to all the sentry posts in St. Petersburg. Paid for by the General Staff."

"Nikolai," Yury said almost in a whisper. "Please do me a favor and see what he has there in the cart."

"Look for yourself."

"It's lemonade!" the proletarian said cheerfully, and he kicked the cart with his shiny boot. The bottles inside rattled with a sound like lisping speech. The cart began to move and rolled beyond the lampposts.

"What's this about General Staff? . . . Anyway, that's all a load of nonsense. Go on, go and give the sentries their lemonade. Only be quick about it, you sadist, go on!"

"Don't you worry, gentlemen! We'll give all of Russia its lemonade!"

"Move alo-o-ong," howled Nikolai, pulling himself erect in the saddle.

"Move alo-o-ong," croaked Yury, curling himself up into a grey ball of felt.

The proletarian put his pass in his pocket, took hold of the handles of his cart, and pushed it away into the distance. Soon he dissolved in the fog, then they heard the crunching of glass under wheels, and then there was silence. Another second went by, and a clock in the distance began striking ten. Somewhere between the seventh chime and eighth, hope like a white seagull soared into Nikolai's inflamed and suffering brain:

"Yury, Yury. . . . Have you got any cocaine left?"

"God," Yury mumbled in relief, slapping his pockets. "Well done, Nikolai. . . . I'd completely forgotten about it. . . . There."

"A full spoon . . . I'll give it back, I promise."

"Whatever you say. Hold the reins. . . . Careful, you

blockhead, you'll spill it all. That's right. Apologies for the block-head."

"Accepted. Cover it with your cap, the wind'll scatter it."

Shpalernaya Street crept back into position, listening dumb-founded with its black windows and gateways to the loud conver-sation in the very center of the roadway.

"The important thing about Strindberg is not his so-called democratic spirit, or even his art, even though he is a genius," Yury was saying, gesticulating energetically with his free hand. "The important thing is that he presents a new human type. The present culture is on the verge of annihilation, and like any being that is dying, it is making desperate attempts to survive, produc-ing strange homunculi in the alchemical laboratories of the spirit. The superman is not at all like Nietzche's idea of him. Nature it-self doesn't know him yet, and it's conducting thousands of ex-periments in mixing together masculinity and femininity. Not just the masculine and the feminine, note. Strindberg, if you like, is merely one step, a stage on the way. And that brings us back to Spengler again. . . ."

"Damn it," thought Nikolai, "how can I remember that name?" But he asked about something else instead.

"Listen, do you remember that poem you were reciting? What were the final lines?"

Yury wrinkled up his forehead for a second before he spoke:

"And on we go. And through the evening light
We see the first convulsions of the night."

Л и к а

NOW THAT HER GENTLE breathing has dissolved back into the world—into this cloudy sky and this cold spring wind—and the volume of Bunin lies here on my knees like a heavy brick, I occasionally lift my eyes from the page to look over at her photograph, which has survived by chance, hanging on the wall.

She was much younger than me. We were thrown together by the whim of fate, and I never believed that her attachment to me was any kind of response to my good qualities. Rather, if I might borrow a term from physiology, for her I was the irritant which produced certain reflex reactions which would have remained the same if my place were taken by some research physicist, a corrupt member of the State Duma, or anyone else capable of appreciating her swarthy southern charm and easing the burden of existence so far from her ancient homeland, in this barren northern country where she had been born through some strange misunderstanding. When she buried her head in my chest, I slowly ran my fingers down her neck and imagined another palm on that delicate curve—a hand with pale, slim fingers and a ring with a small skull, or a coarse, hairy hand bearing blue anchors and dates—sliding along her throat just as slowly, and I felt that the change would leave her heart entirely untouched. I never called her by her full name. For me "Veronica" was a botanical term; it summoned up memories from some distant childhood flowerbed of white blossoms with a stifling smell. I only used its last two syllables, which didn't make the slightest difference to her. She wasn't the least bit sensitive to the music of speech, and she had never even heard of her near namesake, the headless, winged goddess of victory.

My friends took an instant dislike to her. Perhaps they could tell that the magnanimity with which they'd accepted her, if only for a few minutes, into their circle, went completely unnoticed. But to expect anything else from Nika would have been as stupid as to expect a pedestrian walking along the sidewalk to feel a sense of gratitude towards the workers who'd laid down the cement. The people who surrounded her were no more than talking cupboards that appeared for some incomprehensible reason and then disappeared for reasons equally incomprehensible. Though Nika had no interest in the feelings of others, she instinctively sensed their attitude to her, and when I had visitors, she would most often get up and go into the kitchen. My friends weren't overtly rude to her, but they made no secret of their disdain when she wasn't around. Not a single one of them, of course, considered her an equal.

"What's wrong?" one of them asked me with an ironical smile. "Can't your Nika even stand the sight of me?" That she really couldn't never crossed his mind. He assumed with odd naïveté that in Nika's heart of hearts she adored and idolized him.

"You haven't got a clue how to train them," another one said in a moment of drunken intimacy. "I'd have her smooth as silk in a week."

I knew that he knew what he was talking about, because his wife had been training him for more than three years—but the last thing I wanted was to be someone's trainer.

Not that Nika was indifferent to her comforts. With pathological regularity she would turn up in the same armchair that I wanted to sit in. But objects only existed for her as long as she was using them, and then they disappeared, probably because she had practically nothing of her own at all. I sometimes thought that she was the exact type the old-style communists had attempted to breed, without the slightest idea of what the result of their efforts might look like. She paid no attention to other people's feelings, not because she had a bad character, but because she often had no idea that these feelings existed. When she accidentally broke an old Kuznetsov porcelain sugar bowl that stood on a cupboard and an hour later, on a sudden impulse, I slapped her for it, Nika simply did not understand why I had hit her. She darted out of the room, and when I went to apologize, she turned her back to me and faced the wall. For Nika the sugar bowl was nothing more than a shiny truncated cone, stuffed full of papers. For me it was a kind of storehouse for all the proofs of the reality of existence which I had gathered through life: a page from a long-destroyed address book with a telephone number which I had never dialed; a ticket to the "Illusion" cinema with the stub still intact; a small photo; and several prescriptions that had never been filled. I was ashamed of hitting Nika, but apologizing would have been stupid. I didn't know what to do, so I addressed her in a complex, rhetorical style:

"Nika, don't be angry. Old junk can have a strange power over a person. To throw out an old pair of broken glasses is to admit that the entire world seen through them is gone forever, or on the contrary, which is the same thing, it doesn't exist yet—that world lies somewhere in the kingdom of imminent non-existence. . . . Nika, if only you could understand me. . . . Fragments of the past become something like anchors binding the heart to things that no longer exist, which in turn demonstrates that what is usually called the heart does not exist either, because—" I glanced down at her and saw that she was yawning. God only knows what she was thinking about, but my words were certainly not penetrating her lovely little head. I might just as well have been talking to the sofa she was sitting on.

That evening I was particularly gentle with Nika, and yet I couldn't rid myself of the thought that for her there was little difference between my hands running over her body and the branches which caressed her sides when we were out walking in the woods. At that time we still took our walks together.

We were together every day, but I was sober-minded enough to realize that we could never be genuinely close. She never suspected that at the very moment she was pressing her lithe body against me, I might be somewhere quite different, I might completely forget that she existed. In the final analysis she was shallow and vain, and her needs were purely physiological: a full belly, a good sleep, and enough physical affection to maintain a sound digestion. She would doze for hours in front of the television, scarcely even glancing at the screen, eating a little now and then (she preferred fatty food), and she was very fond of sleeping. I don't think I ever once saw her with a book. But her youth and natural elegance lent every manifestation of her character an illusory spiritual content. In her animalistic ways (which is all they were if one thought about it) there was some reflected glimmer of a supreme harmony, a glimpse of the elusive goal that art seeks hopelessly to attain. I began to think that this simple life was truly beautiful and meaningful, and that my own life was based on nothing but fictions invented by others. I used to dream of discovering what she thought of me, but it was pointless trying to get any answers out of her, and she kept no diary that I could have read in secret.

Suddenly one day I realized that I was genuinely interested in her world. She had a habit of sitting at the window for long periods, looking down. Once I stood behind her, put my hand on the back of her neck (she trembled slightly, but didn't pull away), and tried to guess what she was looking at and what she made of what she saw.

The scene in front of us was a typical Moscow yard: a sandpit with a couple of children scrabbling in it, a small log playhouse, a horizontal bar on which people beat carpets, a red metal tent-frame made of welded pipes, dumpsters, crows, and a lamp-post. The red metal frame depressed me most of all, probably be-cause in my childhood, on a grey winter day, my spirit had once been crushed by the weight of a huge volume from East Germany devoted to the long-vanished culture of the mammoth-hunters. Theirs was a remarkably durable civilization which existed en-tirely without change for several thousand years some-where in Siberia. The people lived in small, hemispheric houses made of mammoth skins stretched over a framework which pre-cisely reproduced the geometry of the modern red playground structures, but were made of mammoth tusks lashed together in-stead of welded iron pipes. In that big book the life of these hunters—a romantic and entirely inappropriate term for the un-washed scavengers who once a month lured a large, unsuspecting animal into a pit with pointed stakes at the bottom—was de-scribed in great detail, and I was astonished by what I learned about their daily life, their territory, even their faces. Then and there I drew the first logical conclusion of my life: the German artist who illustrated the book must have been a Soviet prisoner. These red hemispheres standing in almost every yard have ever since seemed to me to be an echo of the culture from which we sprang. There was another echo in the small herds of porcelain mammoths that had wandered out of the depths of millenia into the future and on to millions of Russian sideboards. We have other ancestors, too, I thought. For instance the Tripolye people from the age-old steppes who thousands of years ago practiced agriculture and animal husbandry; in their free time they carved small stone figures of naked women with big fat bottoms (large numbers of these "Venuses," as they are now known, have sur-vived) which evidently stood in the icon-corner of every house. We also know that the log houses on their collective farms were laid out according to a strict plan, with a wide main street, and that all the houses in a village were absolutely identical. The little playground log hut that Nika and I were looking at was a remnant of this culture. A little girl in rubber boots had been sitting in there for over an hour. She herself could not be seen, all that was visible were the light blue boots swinging to and fro.

"My God," I thought, holding Nika close, "and how much I could say about the sandpit—and the dumpsters—and the lamppost—"

But all of that would still be my world, which I was thoroughly sick of, and had no way out of. Mental constructs cluster like flies on the surface of any object reflected on the retinas of my eyes. Nika was entirely free of the degrading necessity to connect the flame hovering over a dumpster with the 1773 Fire of Moscow or the burping croak of the satisfied crow beside the grocery store with the ancient Roman omen recorded in "Julian the Apostate." But what, in that case, did her soul consist of?

My brief interest in her inner world, which I could not enter even though Nika herself was entirely in my power, was obviously stimulated by a desire to change, to rid myself of the constant clamor of thoughts which had dug a deep rut out of which they could no longer escape. Nothing really new had happened to me for a long time, and I hoped that by being close to Nika I would be able to discover some new, unfamiliar way of feeling and living. When I confessed to myself that when she gazed out the window she simply saw what was there—that her intellect was not the least bit inclined to journeying through the past and the future, but was quite content with the present—I realized that I was not actually dealing with the real Nika at all, but with a set of my own thoughts. What I saw, and what I would always see, was only my own conception, which had assumed her form. Nika herself, sitting only a foot away, was as inaccessible as the spire of the Kremlin's Spasskaya Tower. Once again I felt on my shoulders the weightless but unbearable burden of solitude.

"You know, Nika," I said, moving away from her, "I don't give a damn why you look out there or what you see."

She looked round at me and then turned back to the window. She was used to my childish outbursts, and what's more, although she would never have admitted it, she didn't give a damn about anything I said either.

I moved rapidly from one extreme to the other. Once convinced that the mystery of her greenish eyes was merely an optical phenomenon, I decided that I knew all there was to know about her; my attachment was diluted by a slight contempt, which I scarcely attempted to conceal, believing that she wouldn't notice it. But soon I felt she was finding the monotonous seclusion of our life irksome, and she was becoming nervous and irritable.

It was spring and I stayed home almost all the time, and she had to stay with me, while outside the window the grass was already green and behind the thin grey film of hazy clouds stretched across the sky, the watery sun was twice its normal size. I don't remember when she first went out for a walk without me, but I do remember how I felt about it. I let her go without any particular feeling of nervousness, fending off the feeble thought that I ought to go with her.

It wasn't so much that I had started to find her company dull, but simply that I had begun to regard her in the same way she had regarded me from the very beginning, the way one regards a chair or a cactus or a round cloud in the sky outside. Usually, in order to maintain the illusion of my former concern, I would see her to the door of the stairwell, mumble something vague to her as she left, and then go back into my apartment. She never used the elevator, but always ran down the stairs with swift, silent steps. I don't think it was out of any kind of physical vanity—she really was so young and full of energy that it was easier for her to dash down the stairs in two minutes, scarcely touching them as she went, than to spend the same amount of time waiting for the arrival of a humming, coffinlike cabin flooded with harsh yellow light, which smelled of urine and glorified "Depeche Mode." (As a matter of fact, Nika was absolutely indifferent to this group and to rock in general; the only music that I can remember arousing her interest was the track on Pink Floyd's *Animals* where a distant synthesizer, like a military truck full of barking electronic dogs, rumbles towards the front line through heavy clouds of hash smoke.)

I was interested in where she went, not interested enough to spy on her, but enough to make me go out on the balcony with my binoculars a few minutes after she left. I never pretended to myself that what I was doing was right. Her simple walks led her along the avenue past intersecting paths, past benches, past a stall selling soft drinks, and past the spiral staircase that led to the special orders department of the grocery store. Then she turned behind a tall green sixteen-storey building, towards the woods beyond the wide dusty vacant lot. After that I lost sight of her. God, how I would have loved to be her just for a few seconds, and see with new eyes everything that I no longer even noticed. Only then did I realize I simply wanted to stop being myself—that is, to stop existing at all. The longing for the new is one of the most common forms assumed by suicidal impulses in our country.

I thought of the English saying, "Everyone has a skeleton in the closet." Something prevents the English, who generally think clearly about things, from proceeding to the final truth. The most terrible thing is that the skeleton in your closet is not just an object you happen to own, but actually your own skeleton, and the "closet" is a euphemism for the body out of which this skeleton will emerge some day when the closet disappears. I never thought of the closet I called Nika as containing any skeleton. I never imagined that she could die. Everything about her contradicted the very meaning of the word. She was life condensed, in the same way as milk can be condensed. One icy winter evening, she went out completely naked onto the snow-covered balcony, when suddenly a pigeon settled on the railing: Nika squatted down, as though afraid of frightening it away, and froze. A minute went by, and as I stood there admiring her swarthy back, I was astonished to realize that she didn't feel the cold, or had simply forgotten all about it.

That was why her death failed to make any particular impression on me. It simply did not fit into the realm of consciousness associated with feelings; it did not become an emotional fact. Perhaps this was some kind of psychological response to the fact that it was all the result of my own actions. I did not kill her, of course, not with my own hands, but it was me who jolted the invisible tram of fate into motion along the rails, even though it only caught up with her many days later. I was to blame for initiating the long chain of events which terminated in her death. That disgusting animal, for some reason known by some as the "Patriot," with his drooling, gaping jaws and slanting, hairy forehead, who was the last thing she saw in this life, was merely the specific form in which her death was realized, nothing more. It is pointless to seek a culprit. Every sentence finds its own executioner, and every one of us is an accomplice in a mass of murders. Everything in the world is interwoven, and the links of cause and effect can never be traced or restored. Who can tell whether or not by giving up a subway seat to some spiteful old woman we have condemned the children of Zanzibar to starvation? The extent of our foresight and responsibility is too limited, and in the final analysis all causes lead back into infinity, to the creation of the world.

It was a day in March, but the winter was still hard. The fog outside the window was black as a sailor's pea jacket, and I could scarcely make out the rusty *zieg heil* of the pile-driving crane looming up on the nearby construction site. When a pile had been smashed into the ground and the rumbling died away, drunken voices and swearing emerged from the fog, dominated by one high, vibrant tenor. Then there was a clanging as they dragged over another metal pile, and the heavy blows rang out again. When darkness came, it was a little easier. I sat in the armchair opposite Nika, who was stretched out on the sofa, and began leafing through a book by Gaito Gazdanov. I was in the habit of reading aloud, and the fact that she never listened did not bother me in the least. The only indulgence I allowed myself was to emphasize the intonation in certain places. "She could not be called secretive, but it required long acquaintance or emotional intimacy in order to discover how her life had been passed, what she liked, what she disliked, what interested her, what she valued the people she encountered. I never heard any utterance from her which defined her attitudes, although I spoke with her on the most various of topics. She usually listened in silence. Over many weeks I learned only a little more about her than in the first days. She had no reason at all to conceal anything from me, it was simply the consequence of her natural reticence, which was bound to appear strange to me. Whatever I asked her, she was reluctant to answer, and this always surprised me. . . ."

Another thing always surprised me: when I thought about it, almost every book and every poem was dedicated to Nika, whatever she might be called and whatever form she might assume. The more intelligent and subtle the artist, the more indecipherable and inaccessible her mystery became. The finest efforts of the finest souls had been spent on storming this silent, green-eyed inscrutability, and all of them had been dashed to pieces against an invisible or simply nonexistent—and therefore truly insuperable—barrier. All that was left of even the brilliant Vladimir Nabokov, who managed at the final moment to take shelter behind his lyrical hero, were two sad eyes and a phallus a foot long (I explained the latter by the fact that he wrote his famous novel a long way from Mother Russia with its metric system). "And slowly making her way through the drunks, always unaccompanied, always alone . . . ," I mumbled in my reverie as I meditated on the mystery of this silence that had captured so many different hearts on its swift journey through the ages. "The Greek divan was fluffy, and the wall was covered in sweeping murals. . . ." I fell asleep over my book, and when I woke up Nika was not in the room.

I had noticed long before that she went out for short periods at night. I thought she needed a brief constitutional stroll before bed or a few minutes' conversation with others like herself who gathered in the circle of light outside the entrance, where there was always music playing on somebody's cassette deck. I think she had a friend called Masha, bright and ginger-haired. I saw them together a couple of times. I had no objection to all of this; I even left the door open so that she would not wake me with her

fumbling in the dark corridor and would know I was aware of her
strolls in the night. The only thing I did feel was my usual jeal-
ousy that some aspects of the world were once again escaping my
grasp. But I never even thought of going out with her, I realized
how out of place I would be in that setting, and I would hardly
find the company very interesting. Even so I still felt slightly offended that she had a circle of acquaintances which was closed
to me.

When I woke with my book on my knee and saw I was alone
in the room, I suddenly wanted to go downstairs for a while and
smoke a cigarette on the bench in front of the entrance. I decided
that if I saw Nika, I would not betray our connection in any way.
Going down in the elevator, I even imagined how she would
tremble when she saw me, but then, noting my indifference, she
would turn back to Masha (for some reason I was sure they would
be sitting together on the bench) and continue the quiet conversation that only they could understand.

There was nobody outside the door, and I was suddenly uncertain that I would meet her. A brown Mercedes sportscar was
parked right beside the bench. I had seen it occasionally on the
streets nearby, and sometimes here in front of the building. It was
clearly the same car, because its license plate was so easy to recognize, KRA or KAM, or something of the sort. There was quiet
music coming from the second floor, the bushes were swaying
gently in the wind, and the snow was gone from the ground.
"Soon it will be spring," I thought. But it was still cold.

When I went back inside, the old woman like a dried rose
who sat at her post by the door raised her eyes to look at me in
disapproval. It was time to lock the front door. Going up in the
elevator, I thought about the old janitors down in the basement,
pensioners on the final shift of the old Party generation, still
holding aloft the final living branch from the withered tree of the
people's unity. From the intense, tragic look in their eyes it was
obvious that they could not drag this branch very much further
into the future, and they had no one to hand it on to. On the land-

ing I stretched for a last time and opened the staircase door to flick away my cigarette butt. I heard strange sounds on the landing below, leaned over the railings, and saw Nika.

Perhaps a person of rather more refined psychology might have concluded that she had chosen this very spot, only a few steps from her own apartment, in order to experience some special kind of pleasure, to take satisfaction in the violation of hearth and home. The thought never entered my head—I knew that would be too complicated for Nika—but what I saw roused an instinctive revulsion in me. The two bodies fused together in convulsive movement under the flickering faulty lamp looked like an animated sewing machine, and the squealing, which could scarcely be taken for human, was like the squeaking of its unoiled gears. I do not know how long I watched all this, a single second or several minutes. Suddenly I was looking into Nika's eyes and of its own accord my hand raised the rusty lid of the trash can, which a moment later smashed against the wall and clattered down onto her head.

I obviously scared them very badly. They dashed down the stairs, and I had time to recognize who Nika had been with. He lived somewhere in our building, and I had seen him several times on the staircase when the elevator was switched off. He had expressionless eyes, vulgar colorless moustaches, and a strong air of self-importance. Once I saw him rummaging in a garbage can, still maintaining that same air; as I walked past he raised his eyes and stared at me. When I had gone a few steps down the stairs and he was sure I was no competition, I heard the rustling of potato peels start up again behind me as he continued his search. I had long suspected that Nika liked his kind, animals in the full sense of the word, and she would always be attracted to them, no matter whom she herself might resemble in the moonlight, or any other light.

She did not really resemble anyone at all, I thought as I opened the door to the apartment. If, when I look at her, she appears like some perfect work of art, then this has something to do with me, and nothing to do with her. All of the beauty I see is contained in my own heart, because that is where I keep the tuning fork with the note against which I measure everything else. Always confusing myself with my own image, I think that I am dealing with something external, but the world around me is only a system of mirrors with various curvatures. We are arranged in a strange fashion, I pondered, we only see what we intend to see, but we see it in the most minute detail (including faces and positions) in place of what we are actually witnessing—like Humbert Humbert, taking the fat social-democratic elbow in the window next door for the knee of his motionless nymphette.

Nika did not come home that night, and early in the morning I locked every lock on the door and left town for two weeks. When I got back I was met by the pink-haired old janitor who glanced at the three other old women sitting in a semicircle round her table on chairs they had brought from their apartments, and then loudly informed me that Nika had been there several times, but had been unable to get into the apartment, and had not been seen now for several days. The old women were staring at me curiously, and I walked on by quickly. Even so I was overtaken at the elevator by a comment on my moral condition. I felt uneasy, because I had absolutely no idea where to look for her, but I was certain that she would come back. I had a lot to do, and I did not think of her again until the evening, but then the telephone rang, and the old janitor woman, having clearly decided to involve herself in my life, informed me that her name was Tatyana Grigorievna and that she had just seen Nika downstairs.

The pavement in front of the building was turning dark under the fine drizzle. By the entrance several girls were jumping over a piece of taut elastic stretched neck-high and shouting rhythmically as they dexterously threw their legs over it. The wind carried a torn plastic bag over my head. Nika was nowhere to be seen. I turned round the corner of the building and went towards the woods hidden behind the houses. I wasn't certain just where I was going, but I was sure that I would meet Nika. When I reached the final house before the vacant lot, the rain had almost stopped. I went round the corner. She was standing in front of the brown Mercedes with that odd license plate. It was parked with dashing style, one wheel up on the sidewalk. The front door was open and behind the windshield a man who looked like the young Stalin dressed in a handsome striped jacket was smoking a cigarette.

"Hi there, Nika!" I said, and stopped.

She glanced at me, but did not seem to recognize me. I leaned forward and rested my hands on my knees. I had often been told that her kind never forgives an insult, but I hadn't taken this seriously, probably because she had always forgiven me before. The man in the Mercedes turned a disdainful glance on me and frowned slightly.

"Nika, forgive me, okay?" I whispered, trying not to take any notice of him, and I held out my hands to her, only too painfully aware of how vulgar this was. I took some comfort in the fact this would hardly be sensed by Nika, or by the Georgian, who had now bared his gold teeth behind the windshield. She lowered her head as though thinking, and suddenly some indefinite detail convinced me that she was about to take a step towards me, a step away from this stolen Mercedes and the driver who was drilling a hole in my head with eyes that perfectly matched the color of the car, and in a few minutes I would bear her in past the old women in our entry. I was already promising myself never to let her go out alone again. Nika was going to take that step towards me, it was as obvious as the falling raindrops, but suddenly she started and dashed off to the side, and I heard a frightened child's voice shouting behind me.

"Stop! Do as you're told! Stop!"

I looked round and saw a huge Alsatian dashing silently over the grass towards us. His master, a boy wearing a cap with an immense peak, was waving the dog's collar and shouting.

"Patriot! Come back! Heel!"

I remember that endless second perfectly: the black body

hurtling over the surface of the grass; the small figure with one arm raised in the air, as though to lash someone with a whip; several motionless passersby looking in our direction. I remember the thought that came to me at that moment: that even children in American caps talk here in foreign slang. I heard a sharp squealing of brakes behind me, and a woman screamed. Even as I searched with my eyes for Nika, I knew what had happened. The car—it was a flashy Lada with bright stickers on the back window, probably—picked up speed again. Evidently the driver was frightened, even though it was not his fault. When I ran over, the car was already out of sight round a bend. Out of the corner of my eye I glimpsed the dog running back to its master. Suddenly several people appeared out of nowhere, gazing in avid fascination at the unnaturally bright blood on the wet road.

"What a swine," I heard a voice with a Georgian accent say behind me. "He just drove on."

"People like that should be shot," said another voice, a woman's. "They've bought up everything, they have—What are you looking at me like that for? I can see you're one of them too. . . ."

The crowd behind me kept growing. Several other voices joined in the conversation, but I wasn't listening anymore. It had started to rain again, and bubbles were drifting across the puddles, drifting like our thoughts and hopes, like our lives. The wind from the woods brought the first smells of summer, filled with an inexpressible freshness which seemed to promise something that had never yet existed. I felt no grief and I was terribly calm, but as I looked at her lifeless, dark form stretched out across the cement, at her body which even after death had retained its mysterious Siamese beauty, I knew that no matter how my life might change, no matter what my tomorrow might bring, no matter what might replace the things I loved and the things I hated, I would never stand at my window holding any other cat.

Mid-Game

THE STRETCH OF SIDEWALK alongside the Hotel National, for the last thirty feet of Gorky-Tverskaya Street, was fenced off by wooden posts strung with small crumpled red pennants that fluttered in the cold January wind. Anyone who wanted to go down into the pedestrian underpass to cross the street, had to step off the curb and walk along the line of parked cars, reading the brightly colored foreign-language insults stuck to the inside of their windshields. Lusya found one decal on a huge streamlined bus particularly offensive—"We show you Europe." "We" was obviously the firm that owned the bus, but who was "you"? Somehow she suspected that "you" wasn't some foreigner wanting a trip abroad, but Lusya herself, and the snow-plastered bus itself was Europe—so very close and at the same time quite inaccessible. A soldier stuck his beaming red face out from behind Europe: he grinned in a manner so precisely in tune with Lusya's thoughts that her instant response was to turn on her heel and go back the way she'd come.

Climbing the steps to the open platform in front of the Intourist, she went over to the stall that sold coffee. Usually it would have taken at least five minutes to get to the front of the jostling line, but today was frosty so there was no one around. Even the plexiglass window was closed. Lusya knocked. The girl who'd been dozing beside the grill stepped up to the counter and glanced with familiar hatred at Lusya's fox-fur coat ("fifteen skins" as her friends called it), the fox-fur hat, and the face with its faint traces of expensive makeup that was looking in at her from the dark, snowy world.

"Coffee, please," said Lusya.

The girl shoved two small metal coffeepots into the layer of sand on the stove, took the money, and asked:

"Isn't it cold out there, working the street all evening?"

"What a bitch," thought Lusya, but she didn't answer back; she just took her coffee and went over to one of the tables.

Not a very good day. In fact, it had been a very bad day, no one but drunken Finns lounging about outside the National, and they looked as though they were fishermen. The one brief prospect had been a skinny white-haired Frenchman with rakish ogling eyes, but after making a couple of passes by Lusya, he'd never actually said anything, just dropped his empty pack of Gitanes by the trash can, stuck his hands into the pockets of his sheepskin coat, and disappeared round the corner. Frost. It was so cold that even the drivers who dealt in cigarettes, condoms, and beer had moved their free economic zone off the street into the narrow lobby of the "National," where they were exchanging good-natured abuse with the jolly doorman:

"You used to be big in the KGB, and now you're shit just like everyone else. . . . Or maybe you've bought up the entire hall. We've got human rights just like everyone else. . . ."

Lusya went in, bought a pack of Salems from some middle-aged guy with a corroded nose, and went back out into the frost. The foreign clientele were all dozing in their rooms or gazing out their windows at the blinking colored lights of the frozen city, apparently without a moment to spare for Lusya's tender young body.

"Maybe I should go over to the Moskva?" Lusya looked disdainfully over at the grey imperial façade decorated with ten-foot-high blue snowflakes on huge white banners. The fabric rippled in the wind, making the snowflakes look like huge blue lice creeping across the cold wall. "But it's dead over there too . . . ," she thought.

The entry of the Hotel Moskva was certainly depressing. The howling wind and snow seemed to threaten that at any moment a group of young men with simple open faces would emerge from behind the columns, wearing army greatcoats and holding back Alsatians on broad leashes. Inside, in the broad marble entrance hall, a crowd of Asian drunks was singing some ancient battle hymn, while a different kind of music—bleating restaurant music—was blaring out on the third floor:

"Whoah-oah, you're in the army now. . . ."

Lusya left her fur coat and hat in the cloakroom, straightened her feather-light sweater with the silver spangles and went up to the second floor. This might not be a hot spot, but last autumn Lusya had pulled a German here for three hundred marks and two "Poison" perfume atomizers. He'd been perfect, some kind of aging commercial traveler with a wedding ring mark running round his hairy third finger, a fat little man who had already wound up his business with the Soviet authorities and was on the lookout for a moderately sweet and vaguely dangerous adventure in this wild northern land. A client like that won't hang around on the steps of the Intourist, he goes to some darker corner like the Moskva, or even the Minsk, because he's afraid of having to pay too much. He's sure not to be infectious, and his demands will be touchingly simple. But he's a rarity, and above all, he's unpredictable. It's like angling.

Lusya got two cocktails, sat at the corner table in the bar, clicked her lighter, and puffed the smoke up towards the ceiling. The place was almost empty. Two navy officers in black uniforms were sitting at the table opposite, both bald, with faces as long as the grave. A yellow cocktail waited untouched in its glass in front of each of them, and a bottle of vodka stood on the floor under the table—they were drinking through a long plastic tube, passing it back and forth with calm, precise movements, no doubt just the way they pressed the buttons and threw the switches on the control panel of their nuclear submarine.

"I'll drink this and then go home," thought Lusya.

A cassette player started up, drowning out the music from the third floor, and Lusya felt a slight shudder run down her spine. It was one of Abba's old songs, that one about a trumpeter, the moon, and so on. Back in '84—or was it '85—they'd played that one all summer long on the old reel-to-reel "Mayak" in the office of the students' construction brigade. Where had it been? Astrakhan? Or Saratov? My God, thought Lusya, with a strange feeling, look where life's dumped me now. If anybody had told me back then, I'd have smacked his face. And it had all just happened, all by itself. Or had it?

"Plea-ea-ease may I invite you?"

Lusya raised her head. One of the navy officers in black was standing in front of her, staring expressionlessly into her face, his long extended arms swaying ever so slightly.

"Where to?" Lusya asked in surprise.

"To dance. Dance is a rhythm. Rhythm brings freedom."

Lusya was about to open her mouth to reply when she surprised herself by nodding and getting to her feet.

The black arms came together behind her back like a lock closing a suitcase and the officer began moving around between the tables, taking small steps, drawing Lusya after him, and trying to press his black uniform jacket close up against her—it wasn't even a proper uniform jacket, more like a schoolboy's jacket, only larger and with epaulettes. The officer moved completely out of time with the music. He obviously had his own little orchestra somewhere inside him, playing music that was slow and heartrending. There was a smell of vodka from his mouth, not a sour, stale smell, but cold, pure, and chemical.

"Why are you so bald?" Lusya asked, maneuvering the officer away a little bit. "You're still young."

"Seven years in a coffin of stee-eel," the officer sang in a quiet voice, raising his voice almost to a falsetto on the final word.

"Are you joking?" Lusya asked.

"In a co-offin," the officer crooned, now pressing against her quite openly.

"You were talking about freedom. Have you really got any idea what freedom is?" Lusya asked, pushing him away. "Have you?"

The officer muttered something unintelligible.

The music came to an end and Lusya unceremoniously detached his arms, went back to her table, and sat down. The cocktail tasted disgusting. Lusya pushed it away and just for the sake of something to do she opened the purse on her knees. Leafing through the pages of the copy of *The Young Guard* beside her compact and her toothbrush (she hid her foreign currency in the magazine because she knew no one would ever bother to open it), she began counting the green five-dollar bills by touch, summoning up in her mind's eye the noble visage of Lincoln and the inscription "legal tender," which she translated into Russian as "legitimate affection." There were only eight bills left, and Lusya decided with a sigh that she'd better try her luck on the third floor, so she wouldn't suffer any pangs of conscience later.

The way upstairs was barred by a thick velvet rope, and a crowd of locals was milling about in front of it, hoping to get into the restaurant. Sitting on a stool in the narrow passage which remained was the headwaiter, dressed in a blue uniform with yellow trim. Lusya nodded to him and, stepping over the rope, went up to the restaurant and turned into the tiled cubbyhole just before the snack bar. There she found a waiter she knew called Seryozha, pouring leftover champagne out of a large number of glasses through a plastic funnel into an empty bottle that was already wrapped in a napkin and standing in an ice bucket.

"Hi, Seryozha," said Lusya, "how's the scene today?"

Seryozha smiled and waved to her. He felt the same disinterested respect and affection for Lusya as a distinguished lathe-operator no doubt feels on Saturday evenings for an acquaintance who is an ace on the milling machine.

"A bunch of crap, Lusya. Two lousy Poles and a Kampuchean. Come in on Friday. The Arab oil sheiks'll be here. I'll sit you next to the sweatiest of the lot."

"I'm afraid of all those Asians," sighed Lusya. "I pulled an Arab once, Seryozha, and you wouldn't believe what it was like. He carried this damask steel saber around in his suitcase, it folds up like, like a . . ."—Lusya demonstrated with her hands.

"A belt," Sergei suggested.

"No, not a belt, it's . . . like a folding ruler. He couldn't get it up without that saber. Didn't let go of it all night long, even sliced a pillow in half. In the morning I was covered in fluff. Good thing they have bathrooms *en suite.* . . ."

Seryozha laughed, picked up the tray with the champagne bucket, and dashed off into the dining hall. Lusya lingered for a moment by the marble railing to take a look at the decorated ceiling—the center was occupied by a huge fresco, which Lusya vaguely suspected showed the creation of the world in which she'd been born and grown up, and which had somehow totally disappeared during the last few years. At the very center ceremonial fireworks blossomed into vast bouquets, and at the corners Titans stood on guard, maybe skiers in track suits or maybe students with notebooks tucked under their armpits. Lusya had never taken a close look at them because her attention was entirely absorbed by the bright trails and stars of the fireworks, painted in colors long forgotten, the same colors with which the morning sometimes paints the walls of the old Kremlin: lilacs, pinks, and pale purples that roused memories of objects that had evaporated with the mists of time past—caramel tins, tooth powder, and ancient calendars that a forgotten grandmother had left behind with her bundle of share certificates.

The sight of this fresco always made Lusya feel sad. The place often induced thoughts of the impermanence of existence, and then she remembered her friend Natasha who had found an elderly negro to marry her and had almost had her bags packed when suddenly, instead of in warm, well-fed Zimbabwe, she wound up in a chilly Soviet cemetery. Nobody had any idea who had killed her, but it must have been some kind of maniac, because they found a white chess piece in her mouth—a pawn.

Lusya imagined a snowdrift crusted over with ice, and inside it her corpse, her mouth wedged open with a white pawn, and suddenly she felt afraid to stay in this immense, dirty building with its drunken voices roaring and its dishes clattering.

She walked quickly out of the hall and down the stairs to the cloakroom. Something must have shown in her face, for the head-waiter glanced at her and immediately turned his astonished gaze away. "Calm down, you fool," Lusya told herself, "how are you going to work with thoughts like that in your head? No one's going to kill you." The music from the restaurant was even clearer downstairs than on the third floor, quieter, but clearer.

The singer howled "who-ah, who-ah" yet again, then the door slammed shut and the wind took up the same song.

A girl was standing by the entrance, wearing a black leather jumpsuit and a green woolly cap. From the copy of *The Young Guard* protruding from her pocket, Lusya realized that she was a colleague. She could have guessed even without the hint of the journal.

"Got a cigarette?" the girl asked.

Lusya gave her one and the girl lit up.

"Any action in there?" she asked.

"Nothing doing," Lusya answered, "drunken sailors and Sovs. Maybe I'll try the Intourist."

"I was just there," the girl said. "There's a raid on, they've picked up Anya again. Her Cuban general gave her some cocaine and the stupid cow felt so good she decided to tip a waiter twenty dollars, only it turned out the waiter had ideology—he got shell-shocked in El Salvador. He said: If I got my hands on you in the jungle, first I'd give you to the boys to play around with and then I'd stick your stupid bare ass in a termite hill. I spilt my blood, he said, and you're a disgrace to the country I spilt it for."

"It's easy enough to see who's the real disgrace to this country. What's bringing them all out of the woodwork? Have the talks in Vienna run into problems again?"

"The talks have nothing to do with it," said the girl. "There's something new going on. Did you hear about Natasha?"

"Which Natasha? The one who got killed, you mean?" Lusya tried to make the question sound casual.

"Right. The one they dumped in a snowdrift with a pawn in her mouth."

"I heard. What about it?"

"Well, the day before yesterday they found Tanya Polikarpova by the Cosmos hotel, with a rook."

"Tanya's been taken out?" Lusya felt herself turn cold. "Is it state security? Or the mafia?"

"Don't know, don't know," the girl answered thoughtfully. "But it doesn't look like it. They didn't take her dollars, or her groceries either. Just stuck this rook in her mouth. Anyway, no point in talking about it now, with the night still ahead. . . ."

Lusya reached nervously for a cigarette.

"What's your name?" she asked.

"Nelly," the girl replied, "and you're Lusya, I know. Anya was talking about you today."

Lusya looked at her companion more closely. Those dimples on the cheeks, that slightly turned-up nose, the black mascara—it seemed to Lusya that she'd seen the face before somewhere, seen it many times.

"Where have I met her before?" Lusya wondered, thinking hard. "Maybe KGB?"

"I mostly work the Cosmos," said Nelly, as though reading Lusya's thoughts, "but a week ago they changed all the doormen. You could be an old hag before you get friendly with the new ones. Yesterday they wouldn't let this French guy in because he'd left his hotel card in his room. He kept yelling at them to look in the register, but he might as well have been talking to the wall. . . ."

Lusya thought she remembered now.

"I've seen you in the National," she said uncertainly, "in the bar. You've got a great dress."

"Which one?"

"Brown and black."

"Ah," Nelly smiled. "Yves Saint Laurent."

"Oh, come off it!"

Nelly shrugged her shoulders. There was an awkward pause, and then a young man who'd been prowling round them for several minutes came a step closer and spoke in a fricative voice with a Ukrainian accent, but enunciating very clearly:

"Hey, you broads, got any greenstuff you want to shift?"

Lusya glanced derisively at his rabbit-skin hat and cheap leather jacket, and only then at his ruddy face with the small reddish moustache and the watery eyes.

"Whoah, bumpkin," she said, "who's been shipping all of you into Moscow? D'you know what we call greenstuff here?"

"What?" the young man asked, blushing through his ruddy complexion.

"Dollars. And we ain't broads, we're girls. Tell your captain his shitty dictionary's ten years out of date."

The young man was about to reply when Nelly interrupted him: "Don't take offence, Vasya. Once upon a time we were all just like you. Here's five dollars, go buy yourself a coffee in the bar."

"You shouldn't have insulted him like that," Nelly said, when the young man had disappeared behind one of the square columns. "That's Vasya, the doorman from the Vnesheconombank. They send him over every week to find out the exchange rate."

"Okay," said Lusya, "Anyway I'm hitting the road. See you around."

"Why don't we go for a drink?"

Lusya shook her head and smiled.

"Naah," she said, "see you around."

By the time she had walked as far as the Manege hall with her arm held out for a taxi, Lusya was seriously cold. Her face and her hands were icy, and as always the freezing weather made her breasts ache. She caught herself wincing with the pain, remembered the wrinkle that was just beginning to trace itself on her forehead, and made an effort to relax her face. A few seconds later the pain passed.

The taxis hurtled by, their small green lamps winking derisively. The taxi drivers mostly dealt in vodka, and only occasionally if the mood was on them would they pick up passengers they liked the look of. Lusya didn't even raise her arm anymore for the yellow Volgas coming towards her, she was waiting for a private car to stop.

She couldn't get the conversation on the steps of the Moskva out of her head. "Tanya's been taken out," she kept repeating senselessly to herself. The meaning of the phrase didn't really penetrate her consciousness. It was getting extremely cold, and her breasts began to hurt again. She could still get to the subway in time, but then she'd have to wander along an ice-covered major road named after some prehistoric monster, alone, in her expensive fur coat, shuddering at the wind's drunken laughter in the huge concrete archways. She'd already made up her mind that that was the way her evening would end, when a small green bus with a double-letter military number pulled up beside her.

The officer at the wheel was her dance partner from the restaurant, but now he was wearing a black greatcoat and a cap with a big tinplate crest, tilted to one side of his head.

"Get in," said the other bald, black figure in the back of the bus. "Don't screw around."

Lusya glanced into the dim back of the bus and was astonished to see Nelly lounging in a relaxed pose on the long side seat, beside the sailor.

"Lusya!" Nelly shouted happily. "Climb in. The sailor boys are cool. They're going to drop me at my place, then where do you want to go?"

"Krylatskoe," said Lusya.

"Krylatskoe too? That means we're neighbors. Come on, get in . . ."

For the second time that day Lusya acted strangely. Instead of telling them all to get lost the way any self-respecting hard-currency girl would, she stooped over and climbed up the steps. The bus immediately shot away, swerved deftly, and went hurtling past the Bolshoi Theatre, the "Children's World" toy shop, the monument to the great artist Dzerzhinsky and his huge workshop, and off into the dark, howling side streets with their half-ruined wooden fences and empty, black, bottomless windows.

"I'm Vadim," said the second bald sailor. "And this (he nodded at the man behind the wheel) is Valera."

"Valer-r-ra," the driver repeated, as though listening to an unfamiliar word.

"Like some vodka?" Vadim asked.

"Okay," said Lusya, "but only through the tube."

"Through what tube?" Nelly asked.

"That's the way they drink it, through a tube," said Lusya, taking the thin, soft end of the tube and holding it to her lips.

It was a difficult and unpleasant way to drink vodka, but even so it was more amusing than swigging from the bottle.

"What a jolly life you do have, girls," Vadim whispered, "and we . . ."

"Yeah, can't complain," Nelly said, "but I'll take mine in a glass, if that's all right."

"We can fix that."

Lusya suddenly noticed that there was music in the bus too, coming from a cassette player on the engine cover beside Valera. It was the Bad Boys Blue. Lusya liked it, not the music itself, of course, but its effect. Gradually her surroundings felt more relaxed and even natural—the dark interior of the mini-bus with the two gleaming maritime skulls, Nelly swinging her leg in time to the melody, the houses flashing past the window, the cars and the people. The vodka began to take effect and the mixture of indefinable sadness and distinct fear that Lusya had carried with her out of the Moskva evaporated. An ordinary girlish fantasy filled her heart and mind, a dream, chaste in its very hopelessness, of a suntanned, kind-hearted American, and suddenly she wanted so much to believe the foreign singer when he said we would have no regrets and we would fly away from here in a time machine, although we've been sitting here being jolted about for so long now on this train to nowhere.

"Train to nowhere . . . Train to nowhere . . ."

The cassette ended.

The mini-bus came out on to a wide road flanked by ice-shrouded trees and fell in behind a truck with the word PEOPLE painted in yellow on its tailgate. There was some iron object rattling about in the back of the truck, and the clanging seemed to rouse Lusya from her doze.

"Where the hell are we going?" she asked abruptly, frightened because the scenes flashing by outside were unfamiliar, and not even much like Moscow.

"Ne-e-ver mind that," said Valera loudly, and both of the girls shuddered.

"It's okay, we've just got to fill the tank," Vadim put in rapidly. "We haven't got enough gas to get to Krylatskoe."

"Do we have to go far?" Lusya asked.

"No, no, there's a gas station not far from here that takes the coupons. . . ."

The word "coupons" finally laid Lusya's fears to rest.

"We serve in the fleet, girls," said Vadim. "In the atomic submarine Tambov. It's just like a great big underwater armored train with a crew that's one big family. Yeah. . . . Seven years we've been there."

He took off his cap and ran his hand over the dully gleaming curve of his skull. The mini-bus swerved off into a narrow side-street with concrete bunkers along its sides. It looked as though they were already out of the city and in the countryside. From up in the sky the stars ogled them with a cold debauched gleam like the eyes of that day's Frenchman, and the roar of the motor suddenly became strangely quiet, or perhaps it was just that the sound of trucks which had been moving along with them had disappeared.

"The ocean," said Vadim, putting his arm round Nelly's shoulders, "is vast. Wherever you look, an endless grey expanse reaches out on every side as far as the eye can see, and up above the distant starry dome of heaven with clouds drifting by. . . . This thick layer of water. . . . The immense space of the underwater heavens, bright green at first, then dark blue, and it goes on and on for thousands of miles. Huge whales, voracious sharks, mysterious creatures of the depths. . . . And just imagine it, hanging there at the center of this pitiless universe is the fragile shell of our submarine, so very, very tiny, if you just stop to think about it . . . the yellow gleam of a porthole, and behind it there's a meeting going on, and Valera's giving the report. And all around—just think of it!—the great, ancient ocean. . . ."

"We're here," said Valera.

Lusya raised her head and looked around. The bus was standing on flat snow-covered ground about forty yards from a deserted main road. The engine died, and it became very quiet. Outside the windows the stars were twinkling menacingly and there was a forest in the distance. Lusya suddenly felt surprised at how bright it was, although there wasn't a single streetlight, and then she thought that the snow was reflecting the scattered stars. The vodka was making her feel comfortable and safe, and the fleeting suspicion that something was wrong rapidly evaporated.

"What d'you mean we're here? Are you joking or what?" Nelly asked roughly.

Vadim took his arm from her shoulders and sat there with his face buried in his hands, giggling quietly. Valera slipped out of the driver's side and a moment later the side door of the bus was whooshed open. Cloud of steams rushed out into the frosty exterior. Valera mounted the steps slowly and solemnly. In the semi-darkness the expression on his face was invisible, but he was holding a "Makarov" pistol, and under his arm he had a large, battered chessboard. Without turning around, he shoved the door shut with his left hand, its rubber seal squeaking from the frost.

He waved to Vadim with his pistol.

Lusya slipped down off the seat, sobering up with terrifying speed, and made her way to the back of the bus. Nelly also started backing away, then she slipped on something and almost fell on Lusya, but managed to keep her feet.

Valera stood on the front platform, gripping the pistol trained on the girls as though supporting himself on a handrail. Vadim stood beside him, took out a pistol with one hand, took the chessboard from Valera with the other, and shook the chess-pieces out onto the engine cover. Then he froze, as though he'd forgotten what to do next. Valera stood there without moving either, and a green lamp on the dashboard flashed insistently between the two black cardboard silhouettes, informing the intelligence that created it that everything was in order in the bus's complex mechanism.

"Come on, boys," Nelly said in a low, gentle voice, "we'll do anything you like, just put the chess set away. . . ."

"Chess!" Lusya repeated to herself, and she finally realized what was happening.

Nelly's words seemed to bring the sailors to life.

"That's it," Valera said, and slipped off the catch on his pistol. Vadim glanced at him and did the same.

"Get on with it," said Valera, and Vadim turned away, put down his Makarov on the engine cover and hunched over a package lying beside the heap of chessmen. Lusya couldn't work out what he was doing: Vadim kept striking matches, gazing at a piece of paper, and bending back down to the brown vinyl engine cover, where ordinary mini-bus drivers keep their book of gas coupons, can of small change, and microphone. Valera stood stock-still, and Lusya suddenly had the idea that his outstretched hand was very tired.

Vadim finally finished his preparations and stepped to the side. Four lighted candles arranged in a square transformed the engine cover into a strange altar. At the center of the square the open chessboard glinted in the light, its black and white armies already deeply engaged. Terror had heightened Lusya's feelings to an extreme pitch, and despite her lifelong indifference to the game of chess, she suddenly felt the full drama of the clash between the two absolutely irreconcilable principles represented by the crude wooden figures on the checkered field.

On the home side of the black pieces stood a small metallic figurine: a thin man wearing a jacket, with his cheeks sucked in and a strand of steel hair falling across his forehead—Lusya recognised Karpov's expressionless face. He was about eight inches tall, but somehow he seemed huge, and the flickering candle flames made him seem alive, as if he were making repeated, meaningless small movements.

"The bowl," said Valera, and Vadim took a small enamelled bowl out from somewhere in the cab. He set it on the floor, then straightened up and once again they both froze.

"Don't do it, boys," Lusya heard herself say in a strange-sounding voice, and realized she'd made a mistake when the two black figures began moving again.

"You," said Valera, pointing at Nelly.

Nelly pointed her thumb at herself as though asking a question, and the two men in black nodded simultaneously. Nelly walked towards them, clutching the strap of her French handbag in her fist and swinging it to and fro pitifully. When she reached the middle of the bus she stopped and glanced at Lusya. Lusya smiled encouragingly, feeling the tears spring to her eyes.

"You," Valera repeated.

Nelly walked on, and stopped when she reached the two figures in black.

"Now, girl," Vadim said in an official tone, "please make a
move for white."

"What move?" Nelly asked. She seemed calm and indifferent.

"You decide."

Nelly looked at the board and moved one of the pieces.

"Now kneel down please," Vadim said in the same tone.

Nelly glanced at Lusya again, crossed herself in the wrong
direction and slowly sank to her knees, tucking the hem of her
skirt to the side. Valera put his pistol away and drew a long awl
out of his pocket.

"Lean over the bowl," said Vadim.

"The bow-owl," said Valera.

Nelly drew her head into her shoulders.

"I repeat, lean over the bowl."

Lusya pressed her eyes closed.

"We're here," Valera said suddenly.

Lusya opened her eyes.

"We're here," Valera repeated, lowering the hand holding the
awl, "that's not the way a knight moves."

"But that doesn't matter," Vadim said reassuringly, taking
Valera by the arm, "it doesn't matter at all. . . ."

"But it does! Do you want him to lose again? Do you? Have
they bought you too?" Valera squealed.

"Calm down," said Vadim, "please. Do you want her to move
again?"

"He'll lose again," said Valera, "and it'll be because of you
again, you stupid bitch."

"Now, my girl," Vadim said in a tense voice, "get up and
make a proper move."

Nelly got up off her knees, looked at Valera and saw the awl
trembling in his hand. After that everything happened very
quickly—Nelly must have finally realized that this was all real.

She grabbed up the metal figurine by its head and brought its cubic pedestal down with a scream on Valera's black cap, and Valera slumped into the pit of the steps down to the front door as though it had all been arranged beforehand.

Lusya covered her ears with her hands, expecting Vadim to start firing his pistol, but he squatted down on his haunches instead and put his hands over his head. Nelly swung the the metal figure once again and Vadim howled in pain—the blow had caught him on the fingers—but he didn't change his position. Nelly hit him again but he went on sitting there, without moving except to cover his damaged hand with the fingers of his other one, and muttering: "Oh, you bitch!"

Nelly was about to swing at him a third time, when suddenly she noticed the pistol that Vadim had left beside the chessboard. She flung the metal figurine to the floor, grabbed the pistol, and pointed it at Valera, who was hidden from Lusya by a metal partition.

"Drop your gun," she said in a hoarse, manlike voice. "Now!"

A sound of fumbling movements came from behind the partition, and then the pistol came flying out—Valera threw it almost up to the ceiling—and landed on the floor. Nelly quickly picked it up and said:

"Now come on out of there! Hands up!"

Two arms in black sleeves appeared above the partition, followed by a bald head and a pair of attentive eyes. Nelly began slowly backing away down the bus to where Lusya stood frozen in fright. Vadim was still squatting on his haunches, pressing his cap to his head as though a gale-force wind were blowing. Valera glanced at the girls, got down on all fours and began gathering up the chess pieces scattered across the floor. He began singing quietly:

"Seven years in a coffin of stee-eel."

Nelly fired both barrels into the ceiling and Valera jerked to his feet and threw his hands up. Vadim merely pulled his head further down into his greatcoat.

"You lousy bastards," said Lusya, gingerly taking hold of the smoking pistol offered to her, and two black rivulets streamed down her cheeks.

"Now you listen to me," Nelly hissed at the two officers in black. "You, don't move, and you," she turned the barrel of her gun on Valera, "get behind the wheel. And if you so much as brake in the wrong place, I'll plug hot lead into your bald patch with this rod, and you'd better believe I mean it. . . ."

The law-enforcement slang had an instant effect on the sailors. Hardly a trace of Vadim's forehead and cap showed above his shoulders, the rest had all retreated under his greatcoat, and Valera actually sat down on the chessboard, knocking over the burning candles, and swung his leg rapidly into the cab. The motor rattled into life and the bus crept out onto the highway.

"Nelly," Lusya said suddenly, "tell him to put on the Bad Boys Blue."

Nelly didn't say anything, but Valera had obviously heard, and the music began to play. Vadim swayed on his haunches. At first he sobbed a few times, then he began howling from deep in his belly and shaking all over, shifting from one row of seats to the next. At one crossroads Valera turned and said to him:

"Stop that whining, you carrion. . . . You're a disgrace to the entire fleet. . . ."

But Vadim carried on sobbing: it wasn't as though he was crying over what had happened, but more as though he was mourning something else, as though he'd just remembered a stamp album he lost in his childhood. Lusya's felt how her woman's heart was moved by him, and then her hand came across the bottle with the tube stuck into it, still lying on the seat.

"That's the house," said Nelly, pointing to a tall sixteen-storey building along the road ahead of them. "Drive to the entrance, Baldy. . . . Open the door."

The door hissed open.

"Are you handing us over to the Commandant's office?" Valera asked. "Or what?"

"You scum—just get lost," said Nelly, "and if I ever. . . . I've never worked for the pigs."

"That's what I meant," Valera reasoned calmly, "the best thing is a civil settlement. What about the pistols?"

Nelly thought for a moment.

"See that snowdrift?" She pointed to a heap of snow about five yards from the bus. "We'll throw them down to you from the window. We don't need any extras on our rap sheet, do we Lusya?"

Lusya nodded in agreement. She was quite calm now; she felt like a heroic little machine gunner.

"Stay in the bus for five minutes, you scum, got it?" Nelly said, when Lusya was already outside. As she got out, Nelly picked up the metal figurine from the floor and tucked it under her arm, and Lusya saw Valera clench his fists tight beside his distorted face as he gave out a quiet groan. Vadim just carried on sitting there with his hands over his head.

They walked backwards all the way to the entrance. The bus's engine was growling softly and through its windows they could see the two motionless black figures.

"Into the elevator, quick," Nelly muttered. Lusya ran after her to the landing in front of the elevators, but then Nelly suddenly dashed back to her mailbox, opened it, took out a fresh copy of *The Young Guard*, then ran back again. The elevator arrived just at that moment, and when its doors closed behind them Lusya relaxed completely for the first time.

"What a day!" she thought, squinting at the small head protruding from behind Nelly's arm.

"Were you really scared?" Nelly asked.

"Just a bit," Lusya answered. "They're a pair of maniacs, they'd have done us in and dumped us in a snowdrift till spring. With pawns in our mouths. Hey, they're the ones who killed Natasha and Tanya. . . . What'd we let them go for?"

"Just look here," said Nelly, opening her new journal at the last page and holding it up in front of Lusya's nose. "See the size of the print run?"

"Well, so?"

"So. Every forest has its own garbagemen. They keep the numbers in balance."

"That very cynical of you," Lusya muttered.

"Life's a cynical business," answered Nelly.

The lift stopped at one of the upper floors, Lusya didn't notice precisely which. The door of the apartment was the only one on the landing not covered in artificial leather, just plain wood. The lock clicked as it opened.

"Come in."

Nelly's apartment was in an extreme state of disorder. The door into the single room was ajar and the light was on—Nelly must have left it on when she went out. There were clothes thrown about everywhere. Bottles of expensive perfume lay around on the floor like vodka bottles in the flat of an alcoholic. Standing on the carpet among the haphazardly scattered magazines (mostly *Vogue*, but there were a couple of *Newsweek*s) there were several ashtrays bristling with butts. On the floor by the wall stood a small Japanese television, with a huge black twin-cassette deck beside it. By the window was a small bookshelf, with at least ten swollen copies of *The Young Guard* standing on it—even in her best times Lusya had never accumulated more than five, and for a moment she felt jealous. There was a sour scent in the air and Lusya immediately recognized it as the smell produced when spilled champagne is left to evaporate for a few days and turns into something like a blob of glue.

Pride of place in the room went to a double bed so huge that at first it could easily be overlooked altogether. On it lay a blue duvet and several flannel sheets in various colors, a gift from fraternal Vietnam.

"She brings them home as well," thought Lusya, looking

carefully at the metal figurine, "so there can't be anything to be afraid of in that. I'm not the only one. . . ."

"Grossmeister Karpov," she read from the small grey piece of paper glued to the cubic pedestal.

Nelly was left wearing a green woollen dress with a thin black belt which went very well with her black hair and green enamel earrings.

"Take your coat off," she said, "I'll be back in a moment."

Lusya took off her fur coat and hat and hung them on the deer antlers that served as a coatrack. She raked in two different slippers, slipped her feet into them, and went into the bathroom, where the first thing she did was to wash away the black cosmetic rivulets on her cheeks. Then she joined Nelly in the kitchen, which was just as untidy and had the same sour smell of stale champagne. Nelly was gathering various bits of food into a plastic bag: two boxes of chocolate marshmallows, a stick of cervelat sausage, a loaf of bread, and several cans of beer.

"For the sailors," she said to Lusya, "to cheer them up a bit. That one that was sobbing on the floor. . . ."

"Vadim," said Lusya.

"That's right, Vadim. There was something something really touching about him."

Lusya shrugged.

Nelly put both pistols in the plastic bag, then weighed the heavy figurine of the great chessplayer in her hand and finally set it on the fridge.

"It can be a souvenir," she said, opening the window.

Thick clouds of steam burst out of the kitchen just as they had out of the bus half an hour before. Down below the bus looked like a green Christmas-tree ornament, and two long shadows swayed across the ground beside it. Nelly tossed out the bag, which shrank as it flew through the air and then thumped down on the snow-covered rectangle of the lawn. The two black figures immediately made a dash for it.

Nelly hastily closed the window and shuddered.

"I'd have thrown a brick at them," said Lusya.

"Never mind," said Nelly. "They'll find this harder to take. Want some tea?"

"A drink would be better," said Lusya.

"Then let's go back in there, and take this guy along with us. . . . I've got half a bottle of Johnny Walker."

Lusya remembered that Johnny Walker had reputedly been the favorite tipple of the deceased comrade Andropov. My God, she thought suddenly, how recent all that was—the snowstorm on Kalininsky Prospect, the struggle for discipline, the gentle face of the young American pioneer girl on the television screen, the slanting blue signature, "Androp," under the typed text of the reply. . . . And what was his harsh soul now whispering to the tender young spirit of Samantha Smith, who outlived him by such a short margin? How fleeting is life, how frail is man. . . .

Nelly was hastily clearing away the overflowing ashtrays, the tights hanging inside-out on the back of the armchair, the grapefruit skins and biscuit crushed into the carpet, and soon the only things left on the floor were a pile of magazines and the iron grandmaster.

"There, that's a bit more civilized. . . ."

Lusya sat down on the edge of the bed and took a gulp from her wide glass. After the vodka from the plastic tube, she didn't even notice the taste, only a slight burning in her throat.

Nelly sat down beside her and fixed her gaze on the small figurine in the center of the carpet.

"You know," she said, "I read this fairy tale in some book or other. Two armies are fighting a battle on a plain, with this huge mountain towering up above them. And up on the summit two wizards are playing chess. When one of them makes a move, one of the armies down below starts moving as well. If he takes a piece, soldiers die down on the plain, and if one wins, then the other's army is wiped out."

"I've seen something like that . . . ," said Lusya. "That's

right, it was in *Star Wars*, the third film, when Darth Vader's fighting that other one on his starship, and it's like the same things happen down on the planet. Are you talking about those two head-cases?"

"I was just thinking," Nelly went on, ignoring Lusya's question, "maybe it's all the other way round?"

"How d'you mean?"

"The other way round. When one of the armies advances or retreats, one of the wizards has to make a move. And when the other wizard's soldiers are killed, he takes one of his pieces."

"I can't see any difference," said Lusya. "It just depends what side you look at it from."

Nelly reached out a hand holding the thin black slab of the remote control towards the television, and multicolored ice-hockey players began flitting silently across the screen.

"So what are the two armies?" Lusya asked. "Good and evil?"

"Progress and reaction," said Nelly, in a tone that made Lusya laugh. "I don't know. Let's watch this, shall we?"

The ice-hockey rink disappeared and a plump man in glasses appeared, standing beside a large wall-mounted chess board.

"Events have taken an unexpected turn in the final stage of the match for the world chess championship," he said, louder and louder—Nelly kept clicking the button on the remote control. "When the game was adjourned Black clearly had the advantage, but a paradoxical move by one of the White rooks has produced an intriguing situation. . . ."

The figures on the board moved with loud thumping sounds from one square to another.

"One of the two officers, I beg your pardon, bishops, that form the foundation of the Black position came under attack, and the threat was actually produced by the challenger himself, who had failed during his time away from the board to analyze all the consequences of an apparently ill-considered move by a White knight."

The screen switched to a close-up of the commentator's fingers and the profile of a white knight.

"Black's white-square bishop has been forced to withdraw . . . ," the figures thumped around the board again, ". . . and the position of the black-square bishop is almost hopeless."

The commentator poked a finger at the white squares on the board and then at the black squares, twirled his hand in the air and smiled sadly. "I hope we shall know how the game ends in time for the evening news bulletin."

The screen was filled with a large field, hemmed in on both sides by long fences running as far as the forest which bounded the field in the distance. At the bottom of the shot there was a stretch of a main road, with the figures of the weather forecast crawling slowly along it—most of them beginning with a heavy minus sign that looked like a brick.

"I could just take one of those bricks and smack Valera's bald head with it . . . ," thought Lusya.

"D'you know what that music is?" Nelly asked, moving closer to Lusya.

"No," answered Lusya, moving away, and feeling her breasts beginning to ache again. "They used to play it all the time at the end of the news program, but now they don't use it very often."

"It's a French song called *Manchester-Liverpool.*"

"But those are English cities," said Lusya.

"So what? The song's French. You know—all my life, we've been traveling in this train, I don't remember Manchester and I'll probably never get to Liverpool."

Lusya felt Nelly move closer again, until she could feel the warmth of her body through the fine green wool. Then Nelly put her arm on her shoulder, another indefinite gesture that could have been taken for a simple expression of liking, but Lusya already knew what was coming next.

"Nelly, what are you. . . ."

"Ah, France," Nelly sighed in a barely audible voice, and her arm slipped from Lusya's shoulder to her waist.

The news program finished. Then the screen was occupied once again by the announcer, and then by some run-down workshop with a gloomy-looking crowd of workers in caps standing in the center. A correspondent with a microphone popped up, and a table appeared with portly gentlemen in jackets sitting behind it. One of them looked Lusya straight in the eye, hid his indecently hairy hands under the table, and began speaking.

"Paris . . . ," Nelly whispered in Lusya's ear.

"We shouldn't do this," Lusya whispered, mechanically repeating the words of the talking head on the screen, "the workers will not understand and they will not approve. . . ."

"Then we shan't tell them," Nelly murmured in reply, and her movements became even more shameless. She breathed the bewitching fragrance of "Anais Anais," with perhaps a lingering, slightly bitter note of "Fiji."

"All right then," Lusya thought, with an unexpected sense of relief, "this will be my final examination."

Lusya lay on her back and looked up at the ceiling. Nelly was gazing thoughtfully at her profile, with its delicate covering of powder.

"You know something?" she said after a long silence. "You're my first."

"And you're mine," Lusya replied.

"Really?"

"Yes."

"Does it feel good with me?"

Lusya closed her eyes and nodded ever so gently.

"Listen," whispered Nelly, "will you promise me one thing?"

"Yes," Lusya whispered back.

"Promise me that you won't get up and leave, no matter what I tell you. Promise."

"Of course I promise. You don't have to ask."

"Did you notice anything unusual about me at all?"

"No. You know a lot of militia slang, that's all. But if you work for them, what business is that of mine?"

"Apart from that. Nothing else?"

"No, nothing at all."

"Okay then. . . . No, I can't. Kiss me. . . . That's it. Do you know who I used to be?"

"God almighty, what difference does it make?"

"No, that's not what I meant. Have you never heard about transsexuals? About sex-change operations?"

Lusya was suddenly overwhelmed by a fear even worse than she had felt in the bus, and her breasts began aching terribly again. She moved away from Nelly.

"Yes, what about them?"

"Okay, then just let me finish," Nelly whispered hurriedly, as if she were afraid she wouldn't be given enough time. "I used to be a guy. My name was Vassily, Vassily Tsyruk, Secretary of the Regional Committee of the Young Communist League. I used to go around in a suit with a waistcoat and a tie, holding all sorts of meetings. . . . Personal cases. . . . All those agendas and minutes. . . . And then on the way home, I'd pass this hard-currency restaurant, the fancy wheels, the babes like you, and all of them laughing, and there I was in that shitty suit, with my badge and my moustache, carrying my briefcase, and they're all laughing and going off in their cars, driving off somewhere to enjoy themselves. . . . Never mind, I think. . . . I'll serve my time in the Party, then I'll be an instructor in the City Commit-tee—I had everything going for me. And then, I thought, I'll live it up in restaurants much better than that, I'll go all round the world. . . . And then, out of the blue, I went to this Palestinian friendship evening . . . and this drunken Arab, Avada Ali, threw his glass of tea in my face. . . . And so the Regional Committee started asking me: why are people throwing glasses of tea in your face, Tsyruk? Why do they throw them in your face and not in ours? I got an official reprimand entered in my file. I nearly went insane at the time, and then I saw in the Literary Gazette that this guy, a Professor Vyshnevsky, did operations—for homos, you know, but don't think I was like that, too. . . . I wasn't deviant. I just read that he injected various hormones and changed your psychological makeup, and I was having a real hard time living with my old psychological makeup. So, to cut it short, I sold my old 'Moskvich' and went into the clinic. I had six operations in a row, and they were injecting me with hormones all the time. Then a year ago I left the clinic, my hair had grown already, and everything had changed, I walked along the street and the snow-drifts looked like the cotton wool used to look under the Christmas tree. . . . Then I seemed to get used to it. But just recently I've begun feeling as though everybody's watching me and they all know all about me. So then I met you and I thought I could check to make sure whether I really am a woman or. . . . Lusya, what's wrong?"

Lusya had drawn away, and now she was sitting by the wall, squeezing her knees against her breasts with her arms. For a while neither of them spoke.

"Do I disgust you?" Nelly whispered. "Do I?"

"So you used to have a moustache," said Lusya, pushing aside a lock of hair that had fallen over her face. "Maybe you remember you had an organizational deputy? Andron Pavlov? You used to call him the louse?"

"Yes, I remember," Nelly said, astonished.

"He used to go and fetch your beer, too. And then you opened a personal file on him because of the propaganda display? That time they drew Lenin in gloves and Dzerzhinsky without a shadow?"

"How could you. . . . Louse, is it you?"

"And it was you that made up that name for me—what for? Because I hung on every word you said, and sat up every evening till eleven signing minutes? My God, how different everything could have been. . . . D'you know what I've been dreaming of for the last two years? Driving past your Regional Committee in a Mercedes 500 dressed to the nines and seeing Tsyruk, I mean you, walking along with his little Tartar moustache and his briefcase full of minutes from meetings, just to look at you from my place on the back seat, to glance in your eyes and then look straight through you, at the wall. . . . Not to notice you. D'you understand me?"

"But Andron, it wasn't me. . . . In the Party Bureau Shertenevich said that the deputy for organization had to bear responsibility. . . . It was such a scandal, the oldest party member in the region went crazy, the old fart, when he saw your stand. He was just buying some kefir. . . . No, Andron, honestly—is it really you?"

Lusya wiped her lips with a sheet.

"You got any vodka?"

"I've got some neat alcohol," said Nelly, getting up from the bed, "just a moment."

Covering herself with the crumpled sheet, she ran into the kitchen, and Lusya heard a rattle of plates. Something made of glass fell on the floor and shattered. Lusya coughed and dribbled on the carpet, and then she wiped her lips hard again with the sheet.

A minute later Nelly came back with two cheap glasses half-full of liquid.

"Take that. . . . Regional Committee glasses. . . . I don't even know what to call you. . . ."

"What you used to call me, Louse," said Lusya, and there were tears in her eyes.

"Oh, forget it. You're just like some stupid woman. . . . Here's to our meeting."

They drank.

"D'you ever see any of the old gang?" Nelly asked, after a pause.

"No. I hear rumors, though. Remember Vasya Prokudin from the international section?"

"Yes."

"He's been married to a Swedish guy for more than two years now."

"What? You mean he had the operation too?"

"No. In Sweden you can marry a giraffe if you want to."

"Ughu. I was just thinking. He had terrible pockmarks, and a squint."

"There's no way to understand these foreigners," Lusya said wearily. "They're so spoilt for choice, they just go crazy. Just recently I saw one guy in the metro, about forty years old, face like a brick, hardly any forehead at all, and he had a copy of *The Young Guard* in his bag. So there must be some demand even for that. . . . Hey, listen, do you remember Astrakhan, the building brigade?"

Nelly looked at Lusya tenderly.

"Of course."

"Remember they kept playing the same song over and over again? About the trumpeter? And about dancing under the moon? They were playing it today in the Moskva."

"I remember. I've got it here. Shall I put it on?"

Lusya nodded, got off the bed, threw a sheet over her bare shoulders and went over to the small table. Behind her the music began to play.

"Where did you get the operation done?" Nelly asked.

"In a cooperative," Lusya said, surveying the boxes of French tampons strewn across the table. "Seems they pulled a fast one. Instead of American silicone, they put in some rubbishy Soviet rubber. I used to work the Finns on the railway platform near Leningrad, and I thought I would shatter in the frost. And they hurt a lot of the time, too."

"That's not the rubber. Mine often hurt as well. They say it passes after a while."

Nelly sighed and fell silent.

"What are you thinking about?" Lusya asked after a minute or so.

"Oh, nothing. . . . It's just that sometimes, you know, I still feel as though I'm following the party line. Throwing sausage out of window to sailors. D'you understand? It's just that times have changed."

"Aren't you afraid they might change back again?" Lusya asked. "Honestly, now?"

"Not really," said Nelly. "If they do, we'll just have to cope. We've got plenty of experience to rely on, haven't we?"

The pale dawn of winter spread across the wide open field. A small green bus was driving along the deserted highway. Every now and then the bright red name of a collective farm leapt forward to meet it on a sign by the road, and then a few ugly, crooked little houses would go hurtling by, followed by another sign with the same name, only this time with a thick red line running through it.

There were two naval officers in black inside the bus. One, who was driving, had a bandaged head, on which his cap was balanced with difficulty. The other one, sitting on the seat closest to the driver's cab, had bandages on his hands. His face was puffy from crying and smeared with chocolate. He was leafing through the pages of a thick white copy of *The Young Guard* and grimacing in pain as he read in a loud voice.

"A taste for discipline. Discipline and nobility. Discipline and honor. Discipline as an expression of the creative will. The conscious love of discipline. Discipline is order. Order creates rhythm, and rhythm gives rise to freedom. Without discipline there is no freedom. Disorder is chaos. Chaos is decay. Disorder is slavery. The army is discipline. The important thing, as in the tempering of steel, is not to overheat the metal, and to avoid this it is sometimes allowed to cool off a little. . . ."

The bus swerved sharply, and the officer in the back dropped his magazine.

"What d'you think you're doing?" he asked his colleague. "You losing your grip?"

"How could we let them go . . . ," his colleague groaned. "Now he'll lose. He'll lose to that . . . to that. . . ."

"They let us go," the other sailor replied acidly, hunching over the magazine. "Well, shall I carry on reading?"

"Haven't you recovered yet?"

"No. I'm not even close to recovering."

"Then read about the greatcoat."

"Where's that bit?" the first sailor asked, fumbling with the dirt-stained pages.

"Have you already forgotten, you bitch?" said the second sailor with a twisted smile. "You've got a very short memory."

The first sailor said nothing, and just gave him a glazed and wounded look.

"Start from the word 'Lermontov'," said the second sailor.

"Lermontov," the first sailor began, "once called the long-waisted Chechen coat the finest costume in the world for men. In terms of symbolic significance, the Russian officer's coat may now without hesitation be ranked alongside the Chechen coat. Its form, silhouette, and cut are perfect, and most important of all— a very rare occurrence in history—it became a national symbol following the battles of Borodino and Stalingrad. The artist can trace its silhouette in ancient frescoes. Even if all the designers in the world were set to work, they could not create a more perfect or more noble costume than the Russian greatcoat. As Colonel Taras Bulba would have said, 'Their mousy natures would not be up to the job. . .'."

"It doesn't say 'colonel'," the second sailor interrupted.

"No," said the first sailor, running his eyes over the page, "that word's in a different place: 'A father's behest is a report on how you are living your life. Let us recall Colonel Taras Bulba. Manhood is primarily a moral category. In this. . . .'"

"That's enough," said the second sailor. His face seemed to have lit up from inside at those final words, and the black dots of his pupils shifted confidently from the highway to the moon where it hung, gradually growing paler, over the snowy wall of the forest.

The first sailor put down the magazine on the vinyl surface spattered with blobs of candle wax, pulled over a box of chocolate marshmallows, and began to eat. Suddenly he started to sob.

"I always listen to what you say," he said, grimacing with the effort to control his face as he wept, "I always have, ever since we were children. I copy everything you do. But you went mad ages ago, Varvara. I can see that now. . . . Just look at us—bald, wearing sailor's vests, drifting around in a sardine-can and always drinking, drinking. . . . And this chess business. . . ."

"But this is a battle," said the second sailor: "a battle, no quarter given. It's hard on me, too, Tamara."

The first officer covered his face with his hands, unable to speak for a few seconds. Gradually he grew calmer, took a marshmallow out of the box, and shoved it whole into his mouth. "How proud I used to be of you! I even felt sorry for my girlfriends who didn't have any older sisters. . . . And I followed you everywhere you went, everywhere, and I did everything you did. . . . And you always act as though you know what we're living for and how we should live our lives. . . . But now I've had enough. Scared to death before every checkup, and then the nights, with that awl. . . . No, I'm quitting. I've had it."

"And what about our cause?" asked the second sailor.

"What about it? If you really want to know, I don't give a shit about chess."

The bus swerved again, and almost ran into a snowdrift at the roadside. The second officer grabbed hold of a handrail with his bandaged hands and howled in pain.

"No more! I've had it!" shouted the first one. "From now on I'm thinking for myself. You can go back to your Tambov. D'you hear me? Stop the bus!"

Collapsing back into bitter sobbing, he took several IDs of various colors out of his pocket and threw them down on the brown vinyl. The pistol followed them.

"Stop, you pig!" he shouted. "Stop, or I'll jump while we're moving!"

The bus braked and the front door opened. The officer leapt out on to the road with a wail, clutched to his chest the bag with the cervelat sausage and ran off diagonally across the immense square of virgin snow enclosed by the highway, the forest, and the fences, running towards the forest and the moon, which was already completely white. His movements were awkward, almost elephantine, but he moved quite quickly.

The second sailor silently watched the black figure gradually become a smaller and smaller mark on the smooth white field. Sometimes the figure stumbled and fell, then it got up and ran on. Eventually it disappeared completely, and a small, bright tear rolled down the cheek of the sailor sitting at the steering wheel.

The bus started moving. The officer's face gradually recovered its calm expression. The teardrop trembling on his chin dropped on to his uniform jacket and the track it had left on his face dried out.

"Seven years in a coffin of stee-eel," he sang quietly in greeting to the new day and the open road, as wide as life itself.

The Life and Adventures of Shed Number XII

IN THE BEGINNING WAS THE word, and maybe not even just one, but what could he know about that? What he discovered at his point of origin was a stack of planks on wet grass, smelling of fresh resin and soaking up the sun with their yellow surfaces: he found nails in a plywood box, hammers, saws, and so forth—but visualizing all this, he observed that he was thinking the picture into existence rather than just seeing it. Only later did a weak sense of self emerge, when the bicycles already stood inside him and three shelves one above the other covered his right wall. He wasn't really Number XII then; he was merely a new configuration of the stack of planks. But those were the times that had left the most pure and enduring impression. All around lay the wide incomprehensible world, and it seemed as though he had merely interrupted his journey through it, making a halt here, at this spot, for a while.

Certainly the spot could have been better—out behind the low five-storey prefabs, alongside the vegetable gardens and the garbage dump. But why feel upset about something like that? He wasn't going to spend his entire life here, after all. Of course, if he'd really thought about it, he would have been forced to admit that that was precisely what he was going to do—that's the way it is for sheds—but the charm of life's earliest beginnings consists in the absence of such thoughts. He simply stood there in the sunshine, rejoicing in the wind whistling through his cracks if it blew from the woods, or falling into a slight depression if it blew in from over the dump. The depression passed as soon as the wind changed direction, without leaving any long-term effect on a soul that was still only partially formed.

One day he was approached by a man naked to the waist in a pair of red tracksuit pants, holding a brush and a huge can of paint. The shed was already beginning to recognize this man, who was different from all the other people because he could get inside, to the bicycles and the shelves. He stopped by the wall, dipped the brush into the can, and traced a bright crimson line on the planks. An hour later the hut was crimson all over. This was the first real landmark in his memory—everything that came before it was still cloaked in a sense of distant and unreal happiness.

The night after the painting (when he had been given his Roman numeral, his name—the other sheds around him all had ordinary numbers), he held up his tar-papered roof to the moon as he dried. "Where am I?" he thought. "Who am I?"

Above him was the dark sky and inside him stood the brand-new bicycles. A beam of light from the lamp in the yard shone on them through a crack, and the bells on their handlebars gleamed and twinkled more mysteriously than the stars. Higher up, a plastic hoop hung on the wall, and with the very thinnest of his planks Number XII recognized it as a symbol of the eternal riddle of creation which was also represented—so very wonderfully—in his own soul. On the shelves lay all sorts of stupid trifles that lent variety and uniqueness to his inner world. Dill and scented herbs hung drying on a thread stretched from one wall to another, reminding him of something that never ever happens to sheds—but since they reminded him of it anyway, sometimes it seemed that he once must have been not a mere shed, but a dacha, or at the very least a garage.

He became aware of himself, and realized that what he was

aware of, that is himself, was made up of numerous small individual features: of the unearthly personalities of machines for
conquering distance, which smelled of rubber and steel; of the
mystical introspection of the self-enclosed hoop; of the squeaking in the souls of the small items, such as the nails and nuts
which were scattered along the shelves; and of other things.
Within each of these existences there was an infinity of subtle
variation, but still for him each was linked with one important
thing, some decisive feeling—and fusing together, these feelings
gave rise to a new unity, defined in space by the freshly painted
planks, but not actually limited by anything. That was him,
Number XII, and above his head the moon was his equal as it
rushed through the mist and the clouds. . . . That night was
when his life really began.

Soon Number XII realized that he liked most of all the sensation which was derived from or transmitted by the bicycles.
Sometimes on a hot summer day, when the world around him
grew quiet, he would secretly identify himself in turn with the
"Sputnik" and the folding "Kama" and experience two different
kinds of happiness.

In this state he might easily find himself forty miles away
from his real location, perhaps rolling across a deserted bridge
over a canal bounded by concrete banks, or along the violet border of the sun-baked highway, turning into the tunnels formed by
the high bushes lining a narrow dirt track and then hurtling along
it until he emerged onto another road leading to the forest,
through the forest, through the open fields, straight up into the
orange sky above the horizon: he could probably have carried on
riding along the road till the end of his life, but he didn't want to,
because what brought him happiness was the possibility itself. He
might find himself in the city, in some yard where long stems
grew out of the pavement cracks, and spend the evening there—
in fact he could do almost anything.

When he tried to share some of his experiences with the oc-
cult-minded garage that stood beside him, the answer he received

was that in fact there is only one higher happiness: the ecstatic union with the archetypal garage. So how could he tell his neighbor about two different kinds of perfect happiness, one of which folded away, while the other had three-speed gears?

"You mean I should try to feel like a garage too?" he asked one day.

"There is no other path," replied the garage. "Of course, you're not likely to succeed, but your chances are better than those of a kennel or a tobacco kiosk."

"And what if I like feeling like a bicycle?" asked Number XII, revealing his cherished secret.

"By all means, feel like one. I can't say you mustn't," said the garage. "For some of us feelings of the lower kind are the limit, and there's nothing to be done about it."

"What's that written in chalk on your side?" Number XII inquired.

"None of your business, you cheap piece of plywood shit," the garage replied with unexpected malice.

Of course, Number XII had only made the remark because he felt offended—who wouldn't by having his aspirations termed "lower"? After this incident there could be no question of associating with the garage, but Number XII didn't regret it. One morning the garage was demolished, and Number XII was left alone.

Actually, there were two other sheds quite close, to his left, but he tried not to think about them. Not because they were built differently and painted a dull, indefinite color—he could have reconciled himself with that. The problem was something else: on the ground floor of the five-storey prefab where Number XII's owners lived there was a big vegetable shop and these sheds served as its warehouses. They were used for storing carrots, potatoes, beets, and cucumbers, but the factor absolutely dominating every aspect of Number 13 and Number 14 was the pickled cabbage in two huge barrels covered with plastic. Number XII had often seen their great hollow bodies girt with steel hoops surrounded by a retinue of emaciated workmen who were rolling them out at an angle into the yard. At these times he felt afraid and he recalled one of the favorite maxims of the deceased garage, whom he often remembered with sadness, "There are some things in life which you must simply turn your back on as quickly as possible." And no sooner did he recall the maxim than he applied it. The dark and obscure life of his neighbors, their sour exhalations, and obtuse grip on life were a threat to Number XII: the very existence of these squat structures was enough to negate everything else. Every drop of brine in their barrels declared that Number XII's existence in the universe was entirely unnecessary: that, at least, that was how he interpreted the vibrations radiating from their consciousness of the world.

But the day came to an end, the light grew thick, Number XII was a bicycle rushing along a deserted highway and any memories of the horrors of the day seemed simply ridiculous.

It was the middle of the summer when the lock clanked, the hasp was thrown back, and two people entered Number XII: his owner and a woman. Number XII did not like her—somehow she reminded him of everything that he simply could not stand. Not that this impression sprang from the fact that she smelled of pickled cabbage—rather the opposite: it was the smell of pickled cabbage that conveyed some information about this woman, that somehow or other she was the very embodiment of the fermentation and the oppressive force of will to which Numbers 13 and 14 owed their present existence.

Number XII began to think, while the two people went on talking:

"Well, if we take down the shelves it'll do fine, just fine. . . ."

"This is a first-class shed," replied his owner, wheeling the bicycles outside. "No leaks or any other problems. And what a color!"

After wheeling out the bicycles and leaning them against the wall, he began untidily gathering together everything lying on the shelves. It was then that Number XII began to feel upset.

Of course, the bicycles had often disappeared for certain periods of time, and he knew how to use his memory to fill in the gap. Afterwards, when the bicycles were returned to their places, he was always amazed how inadequate the image his memory created was in comparison with the actual beauty that the bicycles simply radiated into space. Whenever they disappeared the bicycles always returned, and these short separations from the most important part of his own soul lent Number XII's life its unpredictable charm. But this time everything was different—the bicycles were being taken away forever.

He realized this from the unceremonious way that the man in the red pants was wreaking total devastation in him—nothing like this had ever happened before. The woman in the white coat had left long ago, but his owner was still rummaging around, raking tools into a bag, and taking down the old cans and patched inner tubes from the wall. Then a truck backed up to his door, and both bicycles dived obediently after the overfilled bags into its gaping tarpaulin maw.

Number XII was empty, and his door stood wide open.

Despite everything he continued to be himself. The souls of all that life had taken away continued to dwell in him, and although they had become shadows of themselves they still fused together to make him Number XII: but it now required all the willpower he could muster to maintain his individuality.

In the morning he noticed a change in himself. No longer interested in the world around him, his attention was focused exclusively on the past, moving in concentric rings of memory. He could explain this: when he left, his owner had forgotten the hoop, and now it was the only real part of his otherwise phantom soul, which was why Number XII felt like a closed circle. But he didn't have enough strength to feel really anything about this, or wonder if it was good or bad. A dreary, colorless yearning overlay every other feeling. A month passed like that.

One day workmen arrived, entered his defenseless open door, and in the space of a few minutes broke down the shelves. Num-

ber XII wasn't even fully aware of his new condition before his
feelings overwhelmed him—which incidentally demonstrates
that he still had enough vital energy left in him to experience fear.

They were rolling a barrel towards him across the yard. Towards him! In his great depths of nostalgic self-pity, he'd never
dreamed anything could be worse than what had already happened—that this could be possible!

The barrel was a fearful sight. Huge and potbellied, it was
very old, and its sides were impregnated with something hideous
which gave out such a powerful stench that even the workers angling it along, who were certainly no strangers to the seamy side
of life, turned their faces away and swore. And Number XII
could also see something that the men couldn't: the barrel exuded
an aura of cold attention as it viewed the world through the damp
likeness of an eye. Number XII did not see them roll it inside and
circle it around on the floor to set it at his very center—he had
fainted.

Suffering maims. Two days passed before Number XII began
to recover his thoughts and his feelings. Now he was different,
and everything in him was different. At the very center of his
soul, at the spot once occupied by the bicycles' windswept
frames, there was pulsating repulsive living death, concentrated
in the slow existence of the barrel and its equally slow thoughts,
which were now Number XII's thoughts. He could feel the fermentation of the rotten brine, and the bubbles rose in him to
burst on the surface, leaving holes in the layer of green mold.
The swollen corpses of the cucumbers were shifted about by the
gas, and the slime-impregnated boards strained against their
rusty iron hoops inside him. All of it was him.

Numbers 13 and 14 no longer frightened him—on the contrary, he rapidly fell into a half-unconscious state of comradery
with them. But the past had not totally disappeared; it had simply
been pushed aside, squashed into a corner. Number XII's new
life was a double one. On the one hand, he felt himself the equal

of Numbers 13 and 14, and yet on the other hand, buried somewhere deep inside him, there remained a sense of terrible injus-
tice about what had happened to him. But his new existence's
center was located in the barrel, which emitted the constant gur-
gling and crackling sounds that had replaced the imagined
whooshing of tires over concrete.

Numbers 13 and 14 explained to him that all he had gone
through was just a normal life change that comes with age.

"The entry into the real world, with its real difficulties and
concerns, always involves certain difficulties," Number 13 would
say. "One's soul is occupied with entirely new problems."

And he would add some words of encouragement: "Never
mind, you'll get used to it. It's only hard at the beginning."

Number 14 was a shed with a rather philosophical turn of
mind. He often spoke of spiritual matters, and soon managed to
convince his new comrade that if the beautiful consisted of harmony ("That's for one," he would say) and inside you—objec-
tively speaking now—you had pickled cucumbers or pickled cabbage ("That's for two"), then the beauty of life consisted in
achieving harmony with the contents of the barrel and removing
all obstacles hindering that. An old dictionary of philosophical
terms had been wedged under his own barrel to keep it from
overflowing, and he often quoted from it. It helped him explain to
Number XII how he should live his life. Number 14 never did
feel complete confidence in the novice, however, sensing something in him that Number 14 no longer sensed in himself.

But gradually Number XII became genuinely resigned to the
situation. Sometimes he even experienced a certain inspiration,
an upsurge of the will to live this new life. But his new friends'
mistrust was well founded. On several occasions Number XII
caught glimpses of something forgotten, like a gleam of light
through a keyhole, and then he would be overwhelmed by a feeling of intense contempt for himself—and he simply hated the
other two.

Naturally, all of this was suppressed by the cucumber barrel's invincible worldview, and Number XII soon began to wonder what it was he'd been getting so upset about. He became simpler and the past gradually bothered him less because it was growing hard for him to keep up with the fleeting flashes of memory. More and more often the barrel seemed like a guarantee of stability and peace, like the ballast of a ship, and sometimes Number XII imagined himself like that, like a ship sailing out into tomorrow.

He began to feel the barrel's innate good nature, but only after he had finally opened his own soul to it. Now the cucumbers seemed almost like children to him.

Numbers 13 and 14 weren't bad comrades—and most importantly, they lent him support in his new existence. Sometimes in the evening the three of them would silently classify the objects of the world, imbuing everything around them with an all-embracing spirit of understanding, and when one of the new little huts that had recently been built nearby shuddered he would look at it and think: "How stupid, but never mind, it'll sow its wild oats and then it'll come to understand. . . ." He saw several such transformations take place before his own eyes, and each one served to confirm the correctness of his opinion yet again. He also experienced a feeling of hatred when anything unnecessary appeared in the world, but thank God, that didn't happen often. The days and the years passed, and it seemed that nothing would change again.

One summer evening, glancing around inside himself, Number XII came across an incomprehensible object, a plastic hoop draped with cobwebs. At first he couldn't make out what it was or what it might be for, and then suddenly he recalled that there were so many things that once used to be connected with this item. The barrel inside him was dozing, and some other part of him cautiously pulled in the threads of memory, but all of them were broken and they led nowhere. But there was something once, wasn't there? Or was there? He concentrated and tried to

understand what it was he couldn't remember, and for a moment
he stopped feeling the barrel and was somehow separate from it.

At that very moment a bicycle entered the yard and for no
reason at all the rider rang the bell on his handlebars twice. It was
enough—Number XII remembered:

A bicycle. A highway. A sunset. A bridge over a river.

He remembered who he really was and at last became himself, really himself. Everything connected with the barrel dropped
off like a dry scab. He suddenly smelt the repulsive stench of the
brine and saw his comrades of yesterday, Numbers 13 and 14, for
what they really were. But there was no time to think about all
this, he had to hurry: he knew that if he didn't do what he had to
do now, the hateful barrel would overpower him again and turn
him into itself.

Meanwhile the barrel had woken up and realized that something was happening. Number XII felt the familiar current of
cold obtuseness he'd been used to thinking was his own. The barrel was awake and starting to fill him—there was only one answer
he could make.

Two electric wires ran under his eaves. While the barrel was
still getting its bearings and working out exactly what was wrong,
he did the only thing he could. He squeezed the wires together
with all his might, using some new power born of despair. A moment later he was overwhelmed by the invincible force emanating
from the cucumber barrel, and for a while he simply ceased to
exist.

But the deed was done: torn from their insulation, the wires
touched, and where they met a purplish-white flame sprang into
life. A second later a fuse blew and the current disappeared from
the wires, but a narrow ribbon of smoke was already snaking up
the dry planking. Then more flames appeared, and meeting no
resistance they began to spread and creep towards the roof.

Number XII came round after the first blow and realized that
the barrel had decided to annihilate him totally. Compressing his
entire being into one of the upper planks in his ceiling, he could

feel that the barrel was not alone—it was being helped by Numbers 13 and 14, who were directing their thoughts at him from outside.

"Obviously," Number XII thought with a strange sense of detachment, "what they are doing now must seem to them like restraining a madman, or perhaps they see an enemy spy whose cunning pretence to be one of them has now been exposed—".

He never finished the thought, because at that moment the barrel threw all its rottenness against the boundaries of his existence with redoubled force. He withstood the blow, but realized that the next one would finish him, and he prepared to die. But time passed, and no new blow came. He expanded his boundaries a little and felt two things—first, the barrel's fear, as cold and sluggish as every sensation it manifested; and second, the flames blazing all around, which were already closing in on the ceiling plank animated by Number XII. The walls were ablaze, the tarpaper roof was weeping fiery tears, and the plastic bottles of sunflower oil were burning on the floor. Some of them were bursting, and the brine was boiling in the barrel, which for all its ponderous might was obviously dying. Number XII extended himself over to the section of the roof that was still left, and summoned up the memory of the day he was painted, and more importantly, of that night: he wanted to die with that thought. Beside him he saw Number 13 was already ablaze, and that was the last thing he noticed. Yet death still didn't come, and when his final splinter burst into flames, something quite unexpected happened.

The director of Vegetable Shop 17, the same woman who had visited Number XII with his owner, was walking home in a foul mood. That evening, at six o'clock, the shed where the oil and cucumbers were stored had suddenly caught fire. The spilled oil had spread the fire to the other sheds—in short, everything that could burn had burned. All that was left of hut Number XII were the keys, and huts Number 13 and 14 were now no more than a few scorched planks.

While the reports were being drawn up and the explanations were being made to the firemen, darkness had fallen, and now the director felt afraid as she walked along the empty road with the trees standing on each side like bandits. She stopped and looked back to make sure no one was following her. There didn't seem to be anyone there. She took a few more steps, then glanced round again, and she thought she could see something twinkling in the distance. Just in case, she went to the edge of the road and stood behind a tree. Staring intently into the darkness, she waited to see what would happen. At the most distant visible point of the road a bright spot came into view. "A motorcycle!" thought the director, pressing hard against the tree trunk. But there was no sound of an engine.

The bright spot moved closer, until she could see that it was not moving on the surface of the road but flying along above it. A moment later, and the spot of light was transformed into something totally unreal—a bicycle without a rider, flying at a height of ten or twelve feet. It was strangely made; it somehow looked as though it had been crudely nailed together out of planks. But strangest of all was that it glowed and flickered and changed color, sometimes turning transparent and then blazing with an unbearably intense brightness. Completely entranced, the director walked out into the middle of the road, and to her appearance the bicycle quite clearly responded. Reducing its height and speed, it turned a few circles in the air above the dazed woman's head. Then it rose higher and hung motionless before swinging round stiffly above the road like a weather vane. It hung there for another moment or two and then finally began to move, gathering speed at an incredible rate until it was no more than a bright dot in the sky. Then that disappeared as well.

When she recovered her senses, the director found herself sitting in the middle of the road. She stood up, shook herself off, completely forgetting. . . . But then, she's of no interest to us.

The Blue Lantern

THE LANTERN BURNING
outside the window made it almost bright in the dorm. Its light
was blue and lifeless, and if not for the moon, which I could see
by leaning out from the bed a long way to the right, the effect
would have been really sinister. The moonlight diluted the
ghastly glow radiating from the top of the tall pole, making it
gentler and more mysterious. But when I swung out to the right,
two legs of the bed hung in the air for a second, and then
smacked back down hard against the floor, and the dull sound
seemed strangely in keeping with the blue strip of light between
the two rows of beds.

"Stop that," said Crutch, waving a blue fist at me, "we can't
hear."

I began to listen.

"Have you heard the one about the dead town?" Tolstoy
asked.

Nobody answered.

"Well then. This guy goes away for two months on a business
trip. When he comes home, he suddenly notices everyone's
dead."

"What, just lying there on the street?"

"No," said Tolstoy, "they were going to work, talking to each other, lining up. Just the same as before. Only he could see that really they were all dead."

"How did he figure out they were dead?"

"How should I know?" Tolstoy answered. "I didn't figure it out, he did. Somehow or other. Anyway, he decided to pretend he hadn't noticed anything, and went on home. He had a wife, and as soon as he saw her he realized she was dead too. And he really loved her, so then he starts asking her what happened while he was away. And she tells him nothing happened. She can't even understand what he's getting at. Then he decides to tell her everything and he says: 'Do you know you're dead?' And his wife answers: 'Yes, I know. But do you know why there's only dead people around here?' 'No,' he says. Then she asks him again: 'Do you know why I'm dead?' 'No,' he says again. Then she says: 'Shall I tell you?' This scares the guy, but he says: 'Okay, tell me.' And she says to him: 'Because you're a corpse yourself.' "

Tolstoy pronounced the final phrase in such a dry, formal voice we felt something almost like real fear.

"Yeah, a real nice business trip that guy went on. . . ." That was Kolya, still a young boy, younger than the others by a year or two. He didn't actually look younger, because he wore huge horn-rimmed glasses that gave him an air of solid respectability.

"So now you're telling a story," Crutch said to him, "since you spoke first."

"That wasn't the deal today," said Kolya.

"That's always the deal," answered Crutch. "Come on, get on with it."

"Let me tell one," said Vasya. "D'you know the one about the blue fingernail?"

"Of course," said a whisper from the corner. "Everyone knows the one about the blue fingernail."

"Ah, but do you know the one about the red patch?" Vasya asked.

"No, we don't know that one," Crutch answered for all of us. "Let's have it."

"This family moves into an apartment," Vasya began slowly, "and there's this red patch on the wall. The children notice it and call their mother to show her. But their mother doesn't say a thing. Just stands there and smiles. Then the children call their father. 'Look, pa,' they say. But their father's dead scared of their mother. 'Let's go,' he says to them, 'it's none of your business.' And their mother just smiles and says nothing. Then they all go to bed."

Vasya stopped speaking and breathed a heavy sigh.

"Then what?" asked Crutch after a few seconds' silence.

"Then it was morning. In the morning they wake up and they see one of the children is missing. Then the children go over to their mother and ask her: 'Ma, where's our little brother?' And their mother anwers: 'He's gone to grandma's. He's with grandma.' The children believe her. Their mother goes off to work and in the evening she comes home and she's smiling. The children say to her: 'Ma, we're scared!' And she smiles again and says to their father: 'They won't do as I tell them. Give them a good beating!' So their father goes and gives them a good beating. The children even want to run away, but their mother's put something in their supper, so they just go on sitting there and can't get up—"

The door opened, and we all instantly closed our eyes and pretended to be asleep. After a few seconds the door closed. Vasya waited a minute for the footsteps in the corridor to die away.

"Next morning they wake up and another one of the children is missing. There's only one little girl left. She goes and asks her father: 'Where's my middle brother?' And her father answers: 'He's at Young Pioneer camp.' And her mother says: 'You tell anyone and I'll kill you!' She didn't even let the girl go to school. In the evening the mother comes home, and she puts something in the little girl's food again, so she can't stand up. And the father locks the door and windows."

Vasya stopped speaking again. This time no one asked him to go on, and the only sound in the half-light was breathing.

"Then these other people come," he continued, "and they look round the apartment and see it's empty. A year goes by and they move new tenants in. When they see the red patch, they go over and slit open the wallpaper, and the mother's in there, all blue, so bloated with blood she can't get out. She was eating the children, and the father was helping her."

For a long time no one spoke, then someone asked:

"Vasya, where's your mother work?"

"What's it matter?" said Vasya.

"You got a sister?"

Vasya didn't answer, he'd either taken offense or fallen asleep.

"Tolstoy," said Crutch, "give us something else about corpses."

"D'you know how people end up as corpses?" Tolstoy asked.

"Sure," answered Crutch, "they just up and die."

"And then what?"

"Nothing," said Crutch, "like sleep, only you don't ever wake up."

"No," said Tolstoy, "that's not what I mean. D'you know what it all starts with?"

"What?"

"It all starts with people listening to stories about corpses. Then they lie there thinking: why are we listening to stories about corpses?"

Someone gave a nervous giggle, and Kolya suddenly sat up in bed and said very seriously: "Cut it out, guys."

"The-ere," said Tolstoy, pleased with himself. "The main thing is to realize you're already a corpse, and the rest is easy."

"You're a corpse yourself," Kolya snarled hesitantly.

"I'm not denying it," said Tolstoy. "But then you'd better think what you're doing talking to a corpse."

Kolya thought for a while.

"Crutch," he said, "you're not really a corpse, are you?"

"Me? How should I know?"

"How about you, Lyosha?"

Lyosha was Kolya's friend from town.

"Kolya," he said, "you just think it through now. You were living in town, right?"

"Right," agreed Kolya.

"Then suddenly they took you away to this other place, right?"

"Right."

"And suddenly you realize you're lying there with all these corpses and you're a corpse yourself."

"Right."

"Right then," said Lyosha, "just think it over a bit."

"We kept on waiting," said Crutch, "thinking you'd work it out for yourself. In all my death I've never seen such a stupid corpse. Don't you understand why we're all here together?"

"No," said Kolya. He was sitting on the bed with his knees drawn up to his chest.

"We're here to accept you into the company of corpses," said Crutch. Kolya gave out a sound between a mumble and a sob, leapt up off the bed and shot out into the corridor like a bullet. We could hear the swift retreating patter of his bare feet.

"Don't laugh," Crutch whispered, "he'll hear you."

"What's there to laugh at?" Tolstoy asked in a melancholy voice. For a few long seconds there was total silence, then Vasya asked from his corner: "But guys, what if? . . ."

"Oh, can it," said Crutch. "Tolstoy, let's have something else."

"Okay, well the story goes like this," Tolstoy began after a pause. "Some people decided to give this friend of theirs a scare. So they got dressed up as corpses, went up to him and said: 'We're corpses, we've come for you.' He got scared all right and ran off. And they stood there and laughed, and then one of them says: 'Listen, guys, what are we all doing dressed up as corpses?' They all look at him and they can't get what he's trying to say. So he tries again: 'Why are all the live people running away from us?'"

"Well, what of it?" asked Crutch.

"That's it. That's when they all realized."

"What'd they realize?"

"Everything, that's what."

Everything went quiet, then Crutch spoke: "Listen, Tolstoy. Can you tell a story properly or not?"

Tolstoy didn't answer.

"Hey, Tolstoy," said Crutch, "why're you so quiet? You died or something?"

Tolstoy said nothing, and every second his silence grew more and more ominous. I had to say something out loud.

"Do you know the one about the TV show *Time?*" I asked.

"Go on," Crutch said quickly.

"It's not all that frightening."

"Go on anyway."

I couldn't remember exactly how the story I was going to tell ended, but I figured I'd remember in the telling.

"Basically, there's this guy about thirty years old, and he sits down to watch *Time* on TV. He turns on the TV and moves up his armchair to make himself more comfortable. First of all the clock comes on, as usual, and he checks his own clock to make sure it's right. Anyway, then the chimes strike for nine o'clock, and the word 'Time' appears on the screen, only not in white, like it always was before, but in black. Well, he's a bit surprised, but then he thinks maybe they've just designed new titles, and he goes on watching. It's all just the same as ever. First they show some tractor or other, and then the Israeli army. Then they tell everyone some member of the academy or other's died, then they show a bit of sport, and then the weather forecast for the next day. That's all. So *Time* is over, and the guy tries to get up out of his armchair—"

"Remind me later, and I'll tell you the one about the green chair," Vasya put in.

"So he wants to get up out of the chair, but he feels like he can't. All his strength's gone. Then he looks at his hand and he sees the skin's all flabby and wrinkled. He gets scared and makes this mighty effort to get up out of the armchair and go into the bathroom to look in the mirror, but it's real hard for him to walk. . . . Eventually he gets there somehow. He looks at himself in the mirror and sees his hair's all grey, his face is a mass of wrinkles, and he's got no teeth. His whole life's gone by while he was watching *Time*."

"I know that one," said Crutch. "It's just the same as the one where they play football with a hockey puck. This guy watches them playing—"

We heard footsteps out in the corridor and a woman's voice raised in annoyance, and instantly we were silent, and Vasya even began snoring unnaturally. A few seconds later the door swung open and the lights went on in the dorm.

"Right, then, who's the chief corpse around here? You, is it, Tolstenko? Antonina Vasilievna was standing in the doorway in her white coat with Kolya beside her, his eyes all red from bawling, trying hard to hide his face behind the radiator.

"The chief corpse in Moscow," Tolstoy answered in a dignified voice, "is on Red Square. And what're you doing waking me up in the middle of the night?"

Such impudence threw Antonina Vasilievna offstride.

"Go in, Averyanov," she said at last, "and lie down. The camp director can sort out the corpses tomorrow. Let's hope they don't all get sent home."

"Antonina Vasilievna," Tolstoy said in a slow drawl, "why're you wearing a white coat?"

"Because that's the way things are done, understand?"

Kolya glanced quickly at Antonina Vasilievna. "Go to bed, Averyanov," she said, "and sleep. Are you a man or not? And as for you. . . ." She turned to Tolstoy. "If you say just one more word, you'll find yourself standing naked in the girls' dormitory. Got it?" Tolstoy stared silently at Antonina Vasilievna's white coat. She looked herself up and down, then looked at Tolstoy and twirled a finger by her ear. But then suddenly she flew into such a fury that her face flushed scarlet. "You didn't answer me, Tolstenko," she said, "d'you realize what'll happen to you?"

"Antonina Vasilievna," said Crutch, "you said yourself that if he said one more word, you'd. . . . How can he answer you?"

"As for you, Kostylev," Antonina Vasilievna said, "the director will have something special to say to you in his office. Remember that."

The light went out and the door slammed shut. For a while, about three minutes maybe, Antonina Vasilievna stood listening outside the door. Then we heard her quiet footsteps along the corridor. There was a loud whisper from Crutch.

"Listen, Kolya, I'll give it to you real good tomorrow. . . ."

"I know," Kolya answered mournfully.

"Oh-h yeah, real good. . . ."

"D'you want to hear about the green chair?" Vasya asked. No one answered. "In this big firm," he began, "there was this director's office with a carpet, a cupboard, and a big desk with a green chair standing in front of it. And in the corner of the office there was this red challenge banner that had been there for ages. And then they appointed this new guy director of the firm. He goes into the office, looks around, and he likes what he sees a lot. So he sits down in the chair and starts working. And then later his deputy comes in and instead of his boss in the chair he sees this skeleton sitting there. Well, they call the police, search everywhere, and they can't find a thing. So then they appoint the deputy to be the director. And he sits down in the chair and starts working.

"They come in later and they see a skeleton sitting in the chair again. They call the police, and they can't find a thing this time either. So they appoint a new director. He already knows what happened to the other directors, and he orders a huge life-size doll. He dresses it in his suit and sits it in the armchair, then he backs off and hides behind the drapes—remind me afterwards, I've just remembered one about yellow drapes—and he waits to see what's going to happen.

"An hour goes by, then another, and suddenly he sees these metal wires come sliding out of the chair and wrap round the doll from all sides. One of the wires goes right round the throat. And then, when the wires have throttled the doll, the red challenge banner comes out of the corner, goes up to the armchair, and covers the doll with its flag. After a few minutes there's nothing left of the doll, and the banner goes back from the desk to its corner. The new director slips out of the room, goes downstairs, takes the fire axe off the wall, goes back into the office, and hacks at the challenge banner with all his might. Then he hears this great groan, and where he split the wooden base in half, blood comes pouring out onto the floor."

"And then what happened?" asked Crutch.

"That's all," answered Vasya.

"And what happened to the guy?"

"They put him away, for the banner."

"And what happened to the banner?"

"They fixed it and put it back," Vasya said, after he paused to think about it.

"And when they appointed a new director, what happened to him?"

"The same thing."

I suddenly remembered that in the camp director's office there were several banners with the numbers of Young Pioneer detachments painted on them. He'd already handed the banners out twice during ceremonial parades. He had a chair in his office, too, but not green, it was red, and it revolved.

"Yeah, I forgot," said Vasya, "when the guy came out from behind the drapes he'd gone completely grey. D'you know the one about the yellow drapes?"

"I do," said Crutch.

"Tolstoy, d'you know the one about the yellow drapes?"

Tolstoy didn't answer.

"Hey, Tolstoy!"

Tolstoy said nothing.

I thought about the fact that I had yellow drapes on my windows in Moscow, yellowish-green anyway. In the summer, when the door of the balcony over the boulevard is open all the time, letting in the noise of the traffic and the smell of exhaust fumes, mixed with something like the scent of flowers, I often sit by the balcony in a green armchair and watch the yellow drapes swaying in the wind.

"Listen, Crutch," Tolstoy said suddenly, "the way people get accepted into the company of corpses is not like you think."

"How is it then?"

"It happens various ways. Only no one ever tells anyone they're joining the corpses. So the corpses don't know afterwards that they're already dead, they think they're still alive."

"So you've already been accepted, have you?"

"I don't know," said Tolstoy, "maybe I have. Or maybe they'll accept me afterwards, when I go back to town. Like I said, they don't tell you."

"Who's 'they'?"

"Who? The dead."

"There you go again," said Crutch. "I wish you'd just shut up. I've had enough."

"S'right," Kolya piped up. "We've had enough."

"As for you, Kolya," said Crutch, "you're still gonna get it good tomorrow."

Tolstoy said nothing for a while, then he started speaking again: "The main thing," he said, "is that even the ones who accept the new ones don't know they're accepting them into the company of corpses."

"How can they accept them then?" asked Crutch.

"Anyway you like. Suppose you just asked someone about something or turned on the TV, and they're really accepting you into the company of corpses."

"That's not what I meant. They must know they're accepting somebody when they accept him."

"Not at all. How can they know anything if they're dead?"

"Then there's no way to understand it," said Crutch. "How can you tell who's alive and who's dead?"

"Why, can't you tell?"

"No," said Crutch, "seems like there's no real difference."

"Well now, just think for a moment about which you are," said Tolstoy. Crutch made a movement in the darkness, and something smacked against the wall just above Tolstoy's head.

"Idiot," said Tolstoy, "you almost hit my head."

"We're dead anyway," said Crutch, "who cares?"

"Hey, guys," said Vasya, "shall I tell you about the yellow drapes?"

"Go screw yourself with your yellow drapes, Vasya. We've heard it a hundred times already."

"I haven't," said Kolya from the corner.

"So what, do we all have to listen to it just for your sake? Then you'll run off crying to Antonina again."

"I was crying because my leg hurt," said Kolya. "I banged my leg on the way out."

"And anyway, you were supposed to be telling a story. You spoke first that time. Did you think we'd forgotten?" said Crutch.

"Vasya told one instead of me."

"He didn't tell one instead of you, he just told one. And now it's your turn. Or else you'll definitely get it good tomorrow."

"D'you know the one about the black hare?" Kolya asked. Somehow I knew straight off which hare he meant: one of the things hanging in the corridor opposite the canteen was a piece of plywood with an image burnt into it of a hare wearing a necktie. Since the drawing had been carefully executed, and in great detail, the hare really did look quite black.

"There, and you said you didn't know any. Let's have it."

"Once there was this Young Pioneer camp. And in the main building there were all sorts of animals drawn on the wall, and one of them was a black hare with a drum. For some reason there were two nails hammered into its paws. Then once this young girl was walking past on her way from lunch to the quiet hour, and she felt sorry for the hare. She went up and pulled out the nails, and suddenly she had the feeling the black hare was looking at her as though it was alive. But then she decided she'd imagined it and went off to the dorm.

"Quiet hour started. And then the black hare suddenly started beating on its drum, and everyone in the camp fell asleep. And they began dreaming that quiet hour was over, that they woke up and went to their afternoon snack. Then it seemed like they did everything the same as usual, played ping-pong, read, and all that stuff. But they were only dreaming it all. Then they all grew up, graduated from school, got married, and began to work and raise children. But in fact they were just sleeping. And all the time the black hare went on beating its drum."

Kolya stopped speaking.

"I don't get it," said Crutch, "you say they all went home. But at home they had parents and friends their own age. Were they dreaming too?"

"No," said Kolya, "they weren't dreaming, they were in the dream."

"What a load of crap," said Crutch. "Did you follow any of that, guys?"

No one answered. It seemed like almost everyone had fallen asleep.

"Tolstoy, did you follow any of that?"

Tolstoy's bed creaked as he bent down to the floor and flung something at Kolya.

"You bastard," said Kolya. "You'll get your face smacked for that."

"Give it back here," said Crutch. It was his running shoe, the one he'd flung at Tolstoy earlier.

Kolya gave him back the shoe.

"Hey," Crutch said to me, "why don't you ever say any-thing?"

"I just feel sleepy," I said.

Crutch curled up in his bed. I thought he was going to say

something else, but he didn't. Nobody said anything. Vasya mumbled something in his sleep.

I looked at the ceiling. Outside, the lantern was swaying on its pole, and the shadows in our dorm swayed in time with it. I turned to face the window. I couldn't see the moon any more. Everything was absolutely quiet, not a sound but the distant drumming of the wheels of a faraway suburban night train. I went on gazing at the blue lantern, and didn't even notice when I fell asleep.

The Tambourine
of the Upper
World

As HE STEPPED INTO THE
vestibule, the soldier glanced in passing at Tanya and Masha before looking over at the corner—then he stopped in his tracks and
stared in astonishment at the woman sitting there.

The woman really did look very odd. Her Mongolian face,
which resembled a three-day-old cafeteria pancake curling up at
the edges, offered absolutely no indication of her age, especially
as her eyes were concealed by ribbons of leather and strings of
beads. Although the weather was warm, she was wearing a fur
hat. It had three wide leather bands. One of them ran round her
forehead to the back of her head, and hanging down from it over
her face, shoulders, and chest were leather braids tied with little
bronze figures, bells, and other charms. The other two leather
bands crisscrossed over the top of her head, where a crudely cast
metal bird perched, stretching its long twisted neck up to the sky.

The woman was dressed in a long broad kaftanlike home-
spun shirt decorated with thin strips of reindeer fur, leather
braiding, small gleaming plates of metal, and lots of little bells
which made a rather pleasant melodic sound at every jolt of the
train. On top all of that, there were numerous small items of obscure significance fastened to her shirt—zigzag iron arrows, two
Medals of Honor, tin faces stamped without mouths, and on her

right shoulder, hanging from a Cross of St. George ribbon, there were two long rusty nails. The woman was clutching an elongated leather tambourine, also decorated with numerous little bells; the rim of another tambourine protruded from the capacious sports bag on which she was squatting.

"Documents," said the soldier at last.

The woman made no response at all to his words.

"She's traveling with me," Tanya put in, "and she hasn't got any documents. And she doesn't understand Russian."

Tanya spoke in the weary voice of someone who has to explain the same thing over and over again, several times a day.

"How's that, no documents?"

"Why should an elderly woman carry any documents around with her? All her papers are in Moscow, in the Ministry of Culture. She's here with a folk-music and dance group."

"Why's she all dressed up like that?" asked the soldier.

"National costume," Tanya answered. "She's an honored reindeer-herder. She has medals for it, see, there, to the right of that bell."

"We're not on the tundra here. This is a breach of social order."

"What order?" said Tanya, raising her voice. "Just what kind of order are you trying to defend? The puddles in the compartments? Or the stench of them?" She nodded towards the door, behind which drunken shouting could be heard.

"We're afraid to sit in the compartment, and instead of keeping order, all you can do is check an old woman's documents."

The soldier looked doubtfully at the woman Tanya had called old. She sat there quietly in the corner of the vestibule, swaying in time with the train, not paying the least attention to the argument being conducted about her. Despite her strange appearance, her small figure radiated such a calm and peaceful energy that when the lieutenant had looked at her for a minute or so he relented: he seemed to smile at something very far away, and his left fist ceased its mechanical chafing of the nightstick hanging from his belt.

"What's her name?" he asked.

"Tyimy," Tanya replied.

"All right," said the soldier sliding the heavy door to the compartment aside. "But just be careful. . . ."

The door closed behind him and the howls from inside the compartment became a little quieter. The local train braked and for a few damp seconds the young women found themselves facing a bumpy asphalt platform, and beyond it low buildings with numerous chimneys of all heights and diameters, some smoking feebly.

"Krematovo station," the loudspeaker announced with a passionless female voice, when the doors had already slammed shut, "Next station—Forty-Third Mile."

"Is that ours?" Tanya asked.

Masha nodded and looked at Tyimy, who was still sitting impassively in the corner. "Has she been with you for long?"

"More than two years now," Tanya answered.

"Is she hard to get along with?"

"Oh, no," said Tanya, "she's very quiet. She sits in the kitchen just like that all the time. Watches television."

"Doesn't she ever go out for a walk?"

"No," said Tanya, "she doesn't go out. She sleeps on the balcony sometimes."

"Does she find it hard? Living in the city, I mean?"

"It was hard for her at first," said Tanya, "then she got used to it. At first she used to bang her tambourine all night long and wrestle with someone invisible. There are lots of spirits in the center. Now it seems they're all her servants. She hung those two nails on her shoulder, see? She defeated them all. But she still hides in the bathroom when there's a firework display."

The Forty-Third Mile station was well suited to its name. Close to a railway station there is usually some kind of human settlement, but here there was nothing except the brick hut of the ticket office, and the only idea with which the place could possibly be associated was its distance from Moscow. The forest began immediately beyond the platform, and it stretched out as far as the eye could see—it was a mystery where the few ragged passengers waiting for a train could have come from.

Masha went ahead, bowed down under the weight of her bag. Tanya walked beside her, carrying a similar bag on her shoulder, and Tyimy brought up the rear, her bells jangling, lifting up the hem of her long shirt when she had to stride across a puddle. She was wearing blue Chinese sneakers and her calves were clad in broad leather leggings embroidered with fine beads. Masha had looked round several times before she noticed that Tiymy had the round dial of an alarm clock sewn to her left legging and a horseshoe fastened to her right legging with a lavatory chain, so that it almost trailed in the mud.

"Listen, Tanya," she asked quietly, "what's she got that horseshoe for?"

"For the Lower World," said Tanys. "Everything there's covered in mud. That's so she won't get stuck."

Masha was going to ask her about the clock face, but she decided not to.

A fine paved road led away from the station into the forest, with old birch trees ranged evenly along both sides, but a thousand or so feet further on all order in the distribution of the trees had disappeared, and then the asphalt imperceptibly petered out and they found themselves slopping through wet mud that sucked at their feet.

Masha thought that once upon a time there must have been a big boss who gave orders for an asphalt road to be laid through the forest, but then since it turned out it wasn't going anywhere in particular, the road was abandoned and forgotten. The sight of it made Masha sad, and her own life, begun some twenty-five years ago through some unknown act of will, suddenly seemed like another road of the same kind: straight and even at first, running between neat, even rows of simple truths, and then—forgotten by some unknown boss—transformed into a crooked track leading God knows where.

Up ahead she caught a glimpse of a piece of white braided cloth tied to a branch of a birch tree.

"Here," said Masha, "we turn right into the forest. About another eighth of a mile."

"That's very close," Tanya said doubtfully, "how could it possibly have survived?"

"No one ever comes here," Masha answered. "There's nothing here, and half the forest is fenced off with barbed wire."

Soon the first low concrete pillar appeared ahead of them, with drooping barbed wire running off both sides. Then a few more pillars came into sight, older and overgrown with dense bushes, so that the barbed wire was invisible until they came really close. The girls walked in silence along the fence until Masha halted at another piece of white braid dangling from a bush.

"Here," she said.

Several strands of the barbed wire had been pulled up and tangled over each other. Masha and Tanya ducked under it without any difficulty, but for some reason Tyimy went through backwards, snagging her shirt. She spent a long time squirming in the gap with her bells jangling.

Beyond the wire the forest was exactly the same; there were no signs at all of human activity. Masha moved ahead confidently, halting after a few minutes at the edge of a ravine with a small stream babbling at its bottom.

"We're here," she said, "it's over there in those bushes."

Tanya looked down. "I can't see anything."

"That's the tail sticking up over there," said Masha, pointing, "and there's the wing. Come on, there's a way down over here."

Tyimy didn't go down, but sat on Tanya's bag, leaned back against a tree, and became perfectly still. Masha and Tanya went down into the ravine, clutching at branches and slipping over the wet earth.

"Tell me, Tanya," Masha said in a quiet voice, "doesn't she need to take a look? How will she manage?"

"Don't worry about that," said Tanya, gazing off into the bushes, "she knows better than we do. . . . She really does. How on earth could this have been preserved?"

Behind the bushes there was something colored a dark dirty brown, extremely old. At first glance it resembled the burial site of a minor nomadic prince who at the very last moment had accepted some strange form of Christianity. A broad cross-shaped twisted metal structure protruded crookedly from a long narrow mound of earth. With an effort it was recognizable as the badly damaged tail of an airplane that had broken away from the fuselage on impact. The fuselage had almost completely sunk into the ground: a few yards ahead of them they could make out among the hazel bushes and the grass the contours of the broken wings, and see a cross on one of them where the dirt had been rubbed away.

"I looked it up in a book," said Masha, breaking the silence, "apparently it's an assault aircraft, a Heinkel. There were two different models, one had a cannon under the fuselage and the other had something else, I don't remember what. Anyway, it's not important."

"Did you open the cockpit?" Tanya asked.

"No," said Masha, "I was too scared to on my own."

"What if there's nobody there?"

"There must be," said Masha, "the glass is intact. Take a look." She stepped forward, pushed aside a few branches, and with the edge of her hand scraped away a layer of humus that had taken years to form.

Tanya bent her face down close to the glass. Beyond it she could see something dark-colored that seemed to be wet.

"How many of them were there?" she asked. "if this is a Heinkel, then surely there should be a gunner too?"

"I don't know," said Masha.

"All right," said Tanya, "Tyimy will find out. It's a pity the cockpit's closed. If we just had a clump of hair or a bone it would make things much easier."

"Can't she manage with this?"

"Yes she can," said Tanya, "only it takes longer. It's starting to get dark already. Let's go collect branches."

"But won't it affect the quality?"

"Quality?" Tanya asked. "What could quality possibly mean in this business?"

The fire was blazing up well and already giving more light than the evening sky covered by low clouds. Masha noticed that she now had a long shadow dancing impatiently across the grass; it upset her that the shadow was clearly so much more confident than she was. Masha felt stupid in her city clothes, but in the flickering firelight Tyimy's costume, which everyone they met during the day had stared at wide-eyed, now seemed like the most comfortable and natural clothing a person could possibly wear.

"Well then," said Tanya, "we'll get started soon."

"What are we waiting for?" Masha asked in a whisper.

"Don't be in such a hurry," Tanya answered just as quietly, "she knows when everything has to be done. Don't say anything to her right now."

Masha sat down on the ground beside her friend. "It's terrifying," she said, running her hand over the spot on her jacket behind which her heart lay. "How long do we have to wait?"

"I don't know, it's always different. Last year there. . . ."

Masha shuddered. The dry note of the tambourine rang out above the meadow, followed by the jangling of many small bells.

Tyimy was standing up, leaning forward, and staring into the bushes at the edge of the ravine. She struck the tambourine again, ran counterclockwise twice round the clearing, leapt the wall of bushes with incredible ease, and vanished into the ravine.

From down below came a pitiful shout filled with pain, and
Masha was sure Tyimy must have broken her leg, but Tanya
merely closed her eyes reassuringly.

They heard quick blows on the tambourine and rapidly
mumbled words. Then everything was quiet and Tyimy emerged
from the bushes. Her movements now were slow and ceremonial.
When she reached the center of the clearing she stopped, lifted
up her hands, and began beating rhythmically on the tambourine.
Just to be on the safe side Masha closed her eyes.

Soon a new sound was added to the beating of the tambourine. Masha didn't notice when it actually began and at first
she couldn't understand what it was: it seemed as though some
unfamiliar string instrument was playing close by, and then she
realized that the piercing hollow note was produced by Tyimy's
voice.

The sound of the voice seemed to exist in some absolutely
separate space, a space which it created and then moved through,
running in its course into many objects of an uncertain nature,
each of which drew from Tyimy several harsh guttural sounds.
For some reason Masha imagined a net dredging across the bottom of a dark pool, gathering in everything in its path. Suddenly
Tyimy's voice snagged on something and Masha could feel her
struggling ineffectively to break free.

Masha opened her eyes. Tyimy was standing quite close to
the fire and trying to pull back her wrist out of empty space. She
was jerking back her arm with all her strength, but the emptiness
would not loosen its grip.

"*Nilti dolgong,*" Tyimy said threateningly, "*nilti djamai!*"

Masha had the distinct feeling that the void facing Tyimy
said something in reply.

Tyimy laughed and shook her tambourine.

"*Nein, Herr General!*" she said "*Das hat mit Ihnen gar nichts
zu tun. Ich bin hier wegen ganz anderer Angelegenheiten.*"

The void asked something and Tyimy shook her head.

"Does she speak German, then?" Masha asked.

"When she's in contact she does," said Tanya. "She can speak any language then."

Tyimy made another attempt to pull her hand free.

"*Heute ist es schon zu spät, Herr General. Verzeihung, ich habe es sehr eilig,*" she shouted in exasperation.

This time Masha could feel the threat from the void.

"*Wozu?*" Tyimy shouted derisively, then tore the Cross of St. George ribbon with the two rusty nails off her shoulder and swung it above her head. "*Nilti djamai! Blyai budulan!*"

The void released her hand so suddenly that Tyimy fell back into the grass. On the ground she started to laugh, then turned to Tanya and Masha and shook her head.

"What's happened?" Masha asked.

"Bad news," said Tanya. "Your client's not in the Lower World."

"Perhaps she didn't look absolutely everywhere?" Masha suggested.

"What everywhere? There isn't any where down there. No beginning to it, and no end."

"So what do we do now?"

"We can try looking in the Upper World," said Tanya. "There's not much chance, it's never worked before. But that's no reason not to try." She turned to Tyimy where she was still sitting on the grass and pointed upwards. Tyimy nodded, went over to the sports bag by the tree and took out the other tambourine. Then she took out a can of Coca-Cola, shook her head, and took a few gulps. Masha was reminded of Martina Navratilova on the center court at Wimbledon.

The Tambourine of the Upper World had a different sound, quieter and more thoughtful. Tyimy's voice was different too, picking out a long mournful note. Instead of fear Masha felt reconciliation and a gentle sadness. The events of a few minutes before were repeated, but this time it was not terrible, it was exalted—and inappropriate. Inappropriate because even Masha realized that there was absolutely no point in disturbing the regions of the world that Tyimy was now addressing with her face turned up to the sky, dark in the spaces between the branches, while she tapped lightly on her tambourine.

Masha recalled an old cartoon about a small grey wolf wandering around in the narrow confined spaces of suburban Moscow, with their daubed, depressing colors. In the animated film all of this sometimes disappeared and out of nowhere would appear an open expanse drenched in midday sunlight, an almost transparent space, with a lightly sketched figure wandering along a pale watercolor road.

Masha shook her head to clear her mind and then looked around.

All the components of her surroundings, all these bushes and trees, the grass and plants and the sky, which only a moment ago had been in direct contact with each other, seemed to have been shaken loose by the music of the tambourine. For a moment a strange, bright, unfamiliar world peeped out through the cracks.

Tyimy's voice snagged against something, tried to move on, and couldn't. It stuck on a single taut note.

Tanya tugged at Masha's sleeve.

"Look, he's there," she said, "We've found him. Now she'll hook him. . . ."

Tyimy raised up her arms, gave a piercing cry, and tumbled over into the grass.

Masha heard a plane rumbling in the distance. Though the sound went on and on, she couldn't make out where it was coming from, and when it stopped she heard a whole series of noises: a blow on glass; a clanging of rusty iron; the quiet but distinct sound of a man coughing.

Tanya got up and took a few steps towards the ravine. Masha spotted a dark figure standing at the edge of the clearing.

"*Sprechen Sie Deutsch?*" Tanya asked in a hoarse voice.

The figure moved silently towards the fire.

"*Sprechen Sie Deutsch?*" Tanya repeated, backing away. "Is he deaf or something?"

The red glow of the fire revealed a stocky man of about forty in a leather jacket and a flying helmet. Moving closer, he sat down opposite the giggling Tyimy, crossed his legs, and looked up at Tanya.

"*Sprechen Sie Deutsch?*"

"Stop saying that, will you," the man replied quietly in Russian, "the same thing over and over."

Tanya whistled in disappointment. "Who are you, then?" she asked.

"Me? Major Zvyagintsev. Nikolai Ivanovich Zvyagintsev. And just who are you?"

Masha and Tanya exchanged glances.

"I don't understand," said Tanya. "What's a Major Zvyagintsev doing in a German plane?"

"A captured plane," said the major. "I was moving it to another airstrip and then. . . ."

Major Zvyagintsev's face contorted, and they could see he'd remembered something extremely unpleasant.

"You mean to say," asked Tanya, "that you're a Soviet flyer?"

"I don't know about that," answered Major Zvyagintsev. "I used to be, but now I'm not sure. Everything's different where I am now."

He looked up at Masha and she looked away, embarrassed.

"What are you doing here, girls?" he asked. "The paths of the living and the dead never cross. Isn't that so?"

"Oh," said Tanya, "please, we're sorry. We never disturb the Soviet flyers. It's all because of the plane. We thought there was a German in it."

"And what do you want with a German?"

Masha raised her eyes and looked at the Major. He had a broad face with a calm expression, a slightly turned-up nose, and several days' stubble on his cheeks. Masha liked faces like that. The Major's appearance was a little spoiled by the bullet hole in his left temple, but Masha had long ago come to the conclusion that there is no such thing as perfection in this world, and she didn't look for it in people—especially not in the way they looked. "It's the times we live in now," said Tanya, "everyone has to earn a crust as best he can. My friend and me. . . ."

She nodded towards the impassive Tyimy.

"Well, let's just say, it's our job. Everybody's leaving nowadays. Marrying a foreigner costs four grand in dollars, and we fix it for about five hundred."

"You mean with dead men?" the major asked incredulously.

"What of it? They still have their citizenship. We bring them back to life on condition that they get married. Usually they're Germans. A German corpse is worth about the same as a live black man from Zimbabwe or a Russian-speaking Jew without a visa. The best catch of all, of course, is a Spaniard from the Blue Division, but that's an expensive kind of corpse. Very rare. There are Italians as well, and Finns. But we don't touch Rumanians or Hungarians."

"So that's it," said the Major. "And do they live very long afterwards?"

"About three years," said Tanya.

"Not very long," said the Major. "Don't you feel sorry for them?"

Tanya thought for a moment. Her beautiful face became quite serious and a deep fold appeared between her eyebrows. The only sound in the ensuing silence was the crackling of twigs in the fire and the quiet rustling of leaves.

"That's straight to the point," she said eventually. "Do you seriously want to know?"

"A hundred and one per cent."

Tanya thought for a little longer. "What I've heard," she began, "is that there's a law of earth and a law of heaven. If you can manifest heavenly power on earth, then all the beings in creation are set in motion and the invisible will be made visible. They have no inner substance—they only consist of a temporary condensation of darkness. That's why, in this constant cycle of transformations, they don't last for long. And since their essence is nothing but void, I don't feel sorry for them."

"That's precisely right," said the Major, "you understand it very well."

The furrow between Tanya's brows relaxed.

"To be honest, most of the time there's so much work that I don't have time to think about it. We usually do about ten a month, less in winter. In Moscow Tyimy's booked in advance for two years."

"And what about the men you bring back to life, do they always agree?"

"Almost always," said Tanya. "It's so terribly dreary there. Dark and crowded, nothing heavenly. The gnashing of teeth. I don't know what it's like where you are, we haven't had any clients from the Upper World. But even down below, of course, the dead are all different. A year ago we had a really terrible case down near Kharkov. Got stuck with this tank driver from the Death's Head Division. We dressed him, washed him, shaved him, explained everything. He said he agreed. His bride was lovely, Marina was her name, from Moscow University. I think she got fixed up with a Japanese sailor afterwards. . . . God, you should see the way they come floating up. . . . Whenever I think about it. . . . What was I talking about?"

"The tank driver," said the Major.

"Oh, yes. Well, to keep it short, we gave him a little money so he would feel at home. So of course he started drinking, they all drink at first. And then in some kiosk they refused to sell him vodka. They wanted roubles, and all he had was coupons and occupation deutsche marks. First he blew away their window with his gun, then he drove in that night on his Tiger and flattened all the kiosks in front of the railway station. Ever since then people keep seeing that tank at night. He drives around Kharkov flattening kiosks. In the daytime he just disappears. No one knows where."

"Strange things like that happen," said the Major, "the world is a strange place."

"Ever since then we only work with the Wehrmacht. We won't have anything to do with the SS. They're all out of their minds. And they don't want to get married, their code won't allow it."

A strong gust of cold wind blew across the clearing. Masha tore her fascinated gaze away from the face of Major Zvyagintsev and saw three shadowy transparent figures emerge from behind a tree standing at the edge of the clearing. Tyimy screeched in fright and instantly hid behind Tanya.

"Here we go," mumbled Tanya. "We're off again. Don't be so afraid of them, you old biddy, they won't touch you."

She stood up and went towards the transparent figures, gesturing reassuringly to them from a distance, just like a driver who has broken a law waves to the soldier who has pulled him over on the highway.

Tyimy huddled up in a tight ball, pressed her head against her knees, and trembled like a leaf. Just to be on the safe side Masha moved closer to the fire and suddenly she felt the full force of Major Zvyagintsev's gaze. She raised her eyes. The Major smiled sadly.

"You're beautiful, Masha," he said in a quiet voice. "When your Tyimy began to call me, I was working in the garden. She called and called until I was really annoyed. I wanted to scare you all away, so I glanced out, and then I saw you, Masha. I was dumbfounded, I don't have the words to express it. In school I had a friend who looked like you—Varya her name was. She was just like you, with the same freckles on her nose. If not for you, Masha, why would I have bothered to come here?"

"You say you have a garden there?" Masha asked, blushing slightly.

"Yes."

"And what's the place where you live called?"

"We don't have any names," said the Major, "and so we live in peace and joy."

"But what's it like there?"

"Fine," said the Major, and he smiled again.

"Well, do you have things, like people do?"

"How can I explain, Masha. We do, but then we don't. Everything's a bit indefinite, a bit vague. But that's only if you start thinking about it."

"Where do you live?"

"I have something like a little house and a plot of land. It's quiet there, very nice."

"Do you have a car?" Masha asked, and then felt embarrassed because her question seemed so stupid.

"If I want one, it's there. Why shouldn't it be?"

"What kind?"

"It varies," said the Major. "And sometimes I have a microwave oven, and what's it called . . . a washing machine. Only there's nothing to wash. And sometimes I have a color television. There's only one channel, but it has all of yours in it."

"Is it a different kind of television every time too?"

"Yes," said the major. "Sometimes it's a Panasonic, sometimes a Shivaki. But when you look very closely, it's gone, nothing but mist hanging in the air. . . . It's like I said, everything's just like it is here, only there aren't any names. Everything is nameless. And the higher you go, the more nameless everything is."

Masha couldn't think of any more questions to ask, so she said nothing and pondered the Major's last words. Meanwhile Tanya was passionately trying to convince the three transparent figures of something.

"I told you already, she's working charms against the thunder," they heard her say. "It's all perfectly legal. When she was a child she was struck by lightning and then the thunder god gave her a piece of tin so she could make herself a visor. . . . What am I supposed to show you? Why should she carry that kind of thing around with her? We've never had this kind of problem before. . . . You should be ashamed of pestering an old woman. You'd be better off sorting out those folk-healers in Moscow. That rotten crap, it's enough to scare you to death, and you come here bothering an old woman . . . I'm going to put in a complaint. . . ."

Masha felt the Major touch her elbow.

"Masha," he said, "I'm going now. I want to leave you something to remember me by."

Masha liked the familiar tone of voice he was using with her now.

"What is it?" she asked.

"A pipe," said the Major. "A reed pipe. Whenever you grow weary of this life, you come to my plane. If you play, I'll come to you."

"And will I be able to visit your home?" Masha asked.

"Yes," said the Major. "You'll eat strawberries. You should see the strawberries I have there."

He stood up.

"Will you come?" he asked. "I'll be waiting."

Masha nodded almost imperceptibly.

"But how can you . . . you're alive now. . . ."

The Major shrugged, took a rusty "TT" revolver out of his leather jacket and set the barrel to his ear.

The shot was like thunder.

Tanya turned round and stared in horror at the Major, who swayed, but remained standing on his feet. Tyimy raised her head and began giggling. There was another gust of cold wind, and Masha saw that the transparent figures were gone from the edge of the clearing.

"I'll be waiting," Major Zvyagintsev repeated and, swaying slightly, he walked over to the ravine, where a faint rainbow radiance hung in the air. A few more steps and his figure dissolved in the darkness, like a sugar lump in a glass of hot tea.

Masha looked out through the train window at the vegetable gardens and little houses rushing past and wept quietly.

"What's wrong, Masha, what is it?" said Tanya, looking into her friend's tearstained face. "Forget it. It happens sometimes. Why don't you come up to Arkhangelsk with the other girls? There's a B-29 in the swamp there, an American 'Flying Fortress.' Eleven men, enough for everybody. Will you come?"

"When did you want to go?" asked Masha.

"Some time after the fifteenth. You should come round on the fifteenth anyway, for the Festival of the Clean Tent. Say you'll come. Tyimy's already dried the toadstools. We'll play the Tambourine of the Upper World for you, since you liked it so much. Tyimy, wouldn't it be great if Masha came round?"

Tyimy lifted up her face and gave a broad smile in reply, revealing brown stumps of teeth protruding in various directions from her gums. The smile looked terrifying because her eyes were concealed by the leather ribbons dangling from her hat—it seemed as though only her mouth was smiling and that the expression in her invisible eyes would be cold and curious.

"Don't be afraid," said Tanya, "she's very kind, really."

But Masha was already looking out the window. In her pocket her fingers were clutching the reed pipe that Major Zvyagintsev had given her and she was thinking very hard.